# COME LET US SING ANYWAY

COME LET US SING ANYWAY

A COLLECTION OF SHORT STORIES

LEONE ROSS

PEEPAL TREE

First published in Great Britain in 2017
Peepal Tree Press Ltd
17 King's Avenue
Leeds LS6 1QS
England

ISBN13: 9781845233341

Supported using public funding by
ARTS COUNCIL
ENGLAND

# CONTENTS

For Soroya and Carol, the keepers of the stories

## LOVE SILK FOOD

Mrs Neecy Brown's husband is falling in love. She can tell, because the love is stuck to the walls of house, making the wallpaper sticky, and it has seeped into the calendar in her kitchen, so bad she can't see what the date is, and the love keeps ruining the food – whatever she does or however hard she concentrates, everything turns to mush. The dumplings lack squelch and bite – they come out doughy and stupid, like grey belches, in her carefully salted water. Her famed liver and green banana is mush too; everything has become too-soft and falling apart, like food made for babies. Silk food, her mother used to call it.

Mrs Neecy Brown's husband is falling in love. Not with her, no.

She gets away from the love by visiting Wood Green Shopping City on a Saturday afternoon. She sits in the foyer on a bench for nearly two hours, between Evans and Shoe Mart. She doesn't like the shoes there; the heels make too much noise, and why are the clothes that Evans makes for heavy ladies always sleeveless? No decorum, she thinks, all that flesh out-of-doors. She likes that word: decorum. It sounds like a lady's word, which suits her just fine.

There are three days left to Christmas and the ceiling of the shopping mall is a forest of cheap gold tinsel and dusty red cartridge paper. People walk past in fake fur hoods and boots. A woman stands by the escalator, her hand slipped into the front of her coat; she seems calm but also she looks like she's holding her heart, below the fat tartan-print scarf around her neck. Then Mrs Neecy Brown sees that the woman by the escalator is her, standing outside her own skin, looking at herself, something her Jamaican granny taught her to do when the world don't feel right. People are staring, so she slips back inside her body and heads home, past a man dragging a flat-faced mop across the mall floor, like he's taking it for a walk.

She trudges through Saturday crowds that are smelly and noisy. The young people have fat bottom lips and won't pick up their feet; she has a moment of pride, thinking of *her* girls. Normal teenagers they'd been, with their moods, but one word from her or one face-twist from Mr Brown, and there was a stop to that! She had all six daughters between 1961 and 1970: a cube, a seven-sided polygon, a rectangle that came out just bigger than the size of her fist and the twin triangles, oh! The two of them so prickly that she locked up shop on Mr Brown for nearly seven months. He was so careful when he finally got back in that their last daughter was a perfectly satisfactory and smooth-sided sphere.

All grown now, scattered across North London, descending on the house every Sunday and also other days in the week, looking for babysitting; pardner-throwing; domino games; approval; advice about underwear and aerated water; argument; looking for Mamma's rub-belly hand during that time of the month; to curse men and girlfriends; to leave pets even though she'd never liked animals in the house; to talk in striated, incorrect patois and to hug-up with their daddy. Then Melba, the sphere, who had grown even rounder in adulthood, came to live upstairs with her baby's father and their two children. The three-year-old sucked the sofa so much he swallowed the pink off the right-hand cushions. The eight-month-old had inherited his father's mosquito face, long limbs and delicate stomach, which meant everyone had to wade through baby sick. Then Lara, Melba's best friend from middle school, arrived in a bomber jacket with a newly-pierced and bleeding lip so long ago that Mrs Neecy Brown didn't even remember when, but regarded her with fond absent-mindedness, not unlike a Christmas decoration you've had so long you don't know where it came from. And the noise. Oh dear, oh Lord.

In between all of this, her husband's bouts of lovesickness.

He'd proved no good at marriage: the repetition, the crying babies, the same good mornings, the perfectly decent night-dresses she bought – *Lord woman, you couldn't try a little harder?* – but there was nothing wrong with her pretty Marks and Spencer cotton shifts, lace at the décolletage, and little cream and brown and yellow and red flowers. He seemed to crave what she privately called The Excitement Girls. She thought of them as wet things: oiled spines, sweating lips, damp laps. She saw one of them once, kissing him goodbye no more than fifteen minutes from their home. She'd scuttled behind a stone pillar to peep. The girl turned away after the kiss. She looked happy. Her chest was jiggling, bra-less, the nipples like bullets.

*So that's what they look like then*, thought Mrs Neecy Brown.

★

She paused at the entrance to Wood Green tube station. One turn to the left and she'd be on her street. No, she wouldn't go home, not yet. He'd be there for his tea, pirouetting through the house with his broad grins and smacking her bottom, his voice too loud. How stupid he thought she was; didn't he know she could see, that she *knew* him? In love he was alternately lascivious and servile and too easily tempted into things – brawls, TV shows, games of poker for too much money. Gone for too long and out too often, and when he came back he would lunge at the family: *Come, let's go to Chessington Park next Sunday, or-we-could or-we-could,* and he'd get his grandchildren excited, and she'd fry chicken and make potato salad and buy Sainsbury's sausage rolls, 39 pence the packet of ten and pack tomatoes like a proper English family, in a proper hamper basket with thermoses of tea. Then, when all is ready, the greatest of apologies he comes up with. Once he even squeezed out tears: *Can't come, Mrs Brown*, he calls her, or *Mummy* on affectionate days, *Can't come, my dears. They working me like a bitch dog, you know. Errol*, she murmurs, *language!* Then he's heading out the house, tripping up on his own sunshine, free, free. *Make sure you come back in time, Errol boy*, she always thinks, *in time to wash that woman's nipples off your neck-back.*

After all.

★

She loves the London underground; it still seems a treat, an adventure, paying your fare, riding the escalator, choosing a seat, settling back to watch the people. So many different kinds, from all over the world! She settles into a corner and watches a Chinese boy struggling with a huge backpack. The straps are caught in his long hair. She'll ride with him all the way to Heathrow, she thinks, see if he untangles the hair before Green Park. Then ride the way back. She leans her head on the glass partition and steps outside of her body.

Last night, Mr Brown did something he'd never done in all these years of his lying, stinking cheating.

Walking in, midnight or thereabouts, easing himself onto the edge of the mattress – she pretending to be asleep as usual, groaning a little, turned on her side – he rolled into the bed, after casting one shoe hither and the other thither and his tongue was in her ear, digging and rooting. Snuffle, snuffle, like a pig. Then she became aware of the smells. Vicks Vapour Rub. Someone else's perfume, and… Mrs Neecy Brown lay trembling and affronted and frozen in the first rage she'd let herself feel for a long time – not since the first time he'd cheated, and repented and wept so much and talked to Pastor for weeks and then just went out and did it again, and she'd realised that it was a habit, this love-falling, and that she could never stop it, only fold her own self into a little twist of paper and stuff herself near the mops and brooms in the downstairs cupboard. No not since then had she let herself cry.

He'd come to her bed unwashed, with the smell of another woman's underneath all over him.

She'd felt as if her head was rising; would never have expected to recognise such an odour so *immediately* when it assailed her. But it was just like the smell of her own underneath, the one that she made sure to clean and dress, like a gleaming, newly-caught fish, lest it flop from between her thighs and swim upriver.

She clapped a hand over her mouth as he snuggled into her, so she didn't leap up and scream it at him: *Is so all woman underneath smell the same, Errol?*

If they were all the same, why turn from her and seek another?

No, she wouldn't cook for him. Let him eat what bits he could find in the fridge for tea, and vex with her. Let him use it as an excuse to storm off to *she*.

★

The Chinese boy has sagged next to the centre pole, holding on for dear life. There are empty seats, but perhaps getting the mammoth backpack off and on makes the option too tiresome. There's another young man sitting to her right. He's wearing a creased blue shirt and stained navy-blue pants. His black socks are covered in fluff, like a carpet that hasn't been hoovered in days. He has a dry, occasional cough and he sits with one hand akimbo, the other on his jaw. His eyes dart around. He's a man in need of a good woman, if ever she's seen one. Then she looks closer and sees she's wrong – someone has creamed his skin and it gleams amongst the other imperfections.

Furthest away are a mother and daughter, stamps of each other, but even if they hadn't been, she would have known. Mothers and daughters sit together in particular ways. Mother is shorter, more vibrant. She rubs her temples, manipulating her whole face like it's ginger dough. Daughter has a face like a steamed pudding, two plaits that begin above her ears and slop straight down over them. Her hand's a wedge of flesh, rubbing her eyes. She smiles at Mrs Neecy Brown, who finds she can't smile back. She can't take the chance. She presumes that Mr Brown finds his girls in north London. He's lazy. This latest one is near, she can feel it;

she could even be this young woman. She wonders whether they know her face, if they've ever followed her.

The train stops, empties, fills, whizzes past stations: Turnpike Lane, Manor House, Finsbury Park, Arsenal, Holloway Road. Where was she, this latest one, casually breaking off bits of her husband and keeping them for herself? She'd had to feed breakfast to a limbless man at least twice; can't forget the week he didn't smile at all because some selfish woman had stolen his lips.

★

She doesn't realise that she's been asleep until she wakes up.

'Hello, ma'am?'

Balding head and a large beauty mark on his left jowl. He hunches forward in the seat; he's been sitting like that for years; she knows the type – bad habits you couldn't break by the time your fifties set in. There's something young about his chin: it's smooth and plump and might quiver when he cries. He's wearing a horrible, mustard-yellow jacket and red trousers.

The man is bending forward, gesticulating, and Mrs Neecy Brown sees that her tartan scarf has fallen to the floor. She leans forward, feeling creaky, bleary, feeling her breasts hang, glimmers at the man who's smiling at her and beats her to it, scooping up the scarf and placing it delicately on her knee, like a present.

'Thank you.'

'You welcome.'

She looks around; they've reached Heathrow. She must have fallen asleep soon after Green Park, half an hour at least! The train hisses. People come in slowly. They'll be heading back soon. She'd like to be a movie star, she thinks – to pack a perfect set of matching luggage and leave the house, a crescent, golden moon above her. She would come to Heathrow and... what? She sighs. The fantasy won't hold. She doesn't have a good suitcase any more, because triangle number one borrowed it and still hasn't given it back, and she knows what that means. Last time she asked for it, the triangle brought her three packs of heavy-duty black garbage bags from Sainsbury's, where she works.

The train jerks and the scarf jolts forward again and spews onto the floor. The man picks it up again, before she can move.

'Look like that scarf don't want to stay with you.'

Sudden rage floods her.

'What you know about me or anything? Mind you bloody business.'

'Oh my,' says the man. He touches a hand to his forehead. 'I'm very sorry, lady.' His voice is slow and wet, like a leaf in autumn. A crushed, gleaming leaf, in shades of gold and red and yellow.

She grunts, an apology of sorts. He recognises the timbre, inclines his head.

She thinks of her girls. If any of them is a cheater, it's the second triangle – with her vaguely cast-eye and that pretty pair of legs. Never could stop needing attention. She sighs. Anger will help nothing.

'You alright, sis?' The autumn man looks concerned.

'What business of yours?'

'Just…' he gestures. 'You look like something important on you mind.'

'Nobody don't tell you that you mustn't talk to strangers on the underground?'

He hoots. 'That is the rule? Well, them tell me England people shy.'

Silence. The train doors close and it starts back home. The man has a suitcase. Marked and scrawled. She remembers arriving in London, so long ago, and how it seemed everything was in boxes: the houses, the gardens, the children and how big and cold the air was and how the colour red snuck in everywhere: double-decker buses and phone boxes and lipstick. Mounds of dog doo on the street, and you could smoke in public places those days. She, a youngish bride, Errol like a cock, waving his large behind and his rock-hard stomach. He'd kicked up dirt in the backyard that he would eventually make her garden and crowed at the neighbours.

Mrs Smith, from two doors down, came to see what the racket was; she brought a home-made trifle and was always in and out after that, helping with the girls, her blonde, cotton-wool head juddering in heartfelt kindness. She'd needed Mrs Smith.

'So you come from Jamaica?' she offers.

'St Elizabeth. Real country.'

'Where you headed?'

The man consults a slip of paper from his lapel pocket. '32 Bruce Grove, Wood Green.'

'Well, that's just near where I am, I can show you.'

They regard each other for some seconds.

'You come to –?'

'You live near –?'

Laughing and the softening of throats, and her hands dance at her neck, tying up the scarf. He has a grin perched on the left hand side of his face.

'Ladies first,' he says.

'You come to see family for Christmas?'

He nods. 'My daughter married an English husband and her child is English. So I come to see them.' He seems to let himself and his excitement loose, slapping his hands on his thighs and humming. 'Yes boy, my first grandchild.'

She smiles. 'I know you have a picture.'

He scrabbles in his wallet and passes it over. His daughter is dark black, big-boned and big-haired, her husband tall and beaming, the child surprisingly anaemic and small-eyed. She has a snotty nose. Mrs Neecy Brown thinks that an English person must have taken the photograph, for anyone else would have wiped it. But they look very happy. Grubby but happy, Mrs Smith would have said. Dead now a year or so. She hands the picture back.

'Pretty.'

He nods vigorously, slaps his thighs again, stows the photo carefully back inside the dreadful coat, blows on his clenched fists. He must be cold, she thinks.

★

Night lies down on Wood Green station as they puff their way up the escalator and stand gazing at the road. My, how they've talked! Not easy; she can't remember the last time she spoke to a man who was listening. The sound of her voice was like a tin, she thought, rattling money. But he'd opened his mouth and made sounds, and so had she, all the way home. The smell of vinegar and chips from a nearby shop; three boys play-wrestle in front of the cinema across the road – some wag had named it Hollywood Green. She doesn't know whether she thinks it's clever or stupid. She points.

'What you think of that name?'

He reads, shakes his head. He doesn't have an opinion. She smiles. That's just fine, with her.

A cat tromps by, meowing. Lord, the noise.

Mrs Neecy Brown drops her handbag and grabs the autumn man's arm, and reaches up to his shoulder, fingers scrabbling, her wedding ring golden against his terrible jacket. She hates cats. They don't seem to care. He puts his suitcase down and pats her hand. They stand like that, arms interlinked, her hand on his shoulder, his hand patting. She is aware of happiness.

Eventually she moves away and he picks up the suitcase. Her fingers tingle from the shape of his shoulder. She waves towards the darkened roads. 'I show you where.'

★

There's mist between them when they find number 32, mist where he's breathing hard from carrying the suitcase. She can see fairy lights in the window of the house and hear the sound of Slade's 'Merry Xmas Everybody' coming from somewhere.

The autumn man rifles in his suitcase. He holds something out to her.

'Some of my wife Christmas cake. She make a good cake, rich. You will like it.'

The tips of her fingers explode as she touches the foil paper. She's aware that her mouth is slightly open. Wife, well. Of course. Wife. He is a big man.

'I must be going now,' she says.

He smiles at her, she smiles back, at this orange man standing in front of a dull wall. A light has come on in the front room; perhaps they've been watching for him.

'Daddy!'

The young woman flings herself forward and he hugs her close.

'Andy, bring Precious! Bring her! Oh no, don't bring her – cold out here. Andy, don't bring her, you hear? We coming in! Come, Daddy!'

Then she sees Mrs Neecy Brown.

'Good evening?' she says. The vowels have slowed and lengthened.

'Good evening,' says Mrs Neecy Brown. There is something moving up and down her back, some unknown discomfort. What is it? The husband has come out of the house now, thinner and better looking than his photograph and he's disobeyed his wife, has a shy child on his hip and the autumn man who has a wife, of course he does, is tousling the child's plaits and the men are pumping hands. *I don't know his name*, thinks Mrs Neecy Brown. She feels absurdly forgotten. Shuffles. The daughter is like a piece of tall, sharp glass. She has thrust the moonlight in the front yard between them.

Oh, glaring.

'Well…' says Mrs Neecy Brown. She shivers; her coat is too thin for this time of the year.

'Well?' says the daughter. The suggestion in her tone is unmistakeable. *Move from my yard and my father, you woman. You Excitement Girl.* She wants to laugh. Could she be that dangerous? Could she be that pulsing sun?

'I – no, no –' she struggles. She tries again. 'You – I –'

'Goodnight, goodnight –' calls the autumn man, who doesn't know her name either and gleams less now. The unknown names might have been romantic in a movie, but, suddenly, Mrs Neecy Brown can only see it as the daughter does: sordid, undignified. Shamed, she lifts her hand to wave, so that it will all be finished, but the men have already turned their backs, heading inside, making the sounds of cockerels at each other, the formerly shy child trilling 'Granddaddy, Granddaddy!'

They are gone.

The daughter growls, like an angry cat.

Mrs Neecy Brown draws herself up and flattens her stomach against her backbone. For after all. Presumption gone too far now.

'I am a *good* woman,' she says, calmly.

The house door clicks shut.

There are Christmas lights and gleaming trees in people's front rooms. She walks slowly, savouring the cold whipping her shoulders. Under the streetlight you can see she's eating another woman's Christmas cake, licking the black, rum-soaked softness off her tingling fingers. Like silk food, her mother used to say.

## ECHO

The young black man dies like a flower. Crumples in red dew. His bloom fades, hand falling to his side, like under rain, his mouth a puzzled 'o' shape. The bullets hover around his head, bees and hummingbirds. He sags. Petals fall. The weight of his body tilts him forward and off the stem.

The little girl standing in the store, watching, will refuse flowers for the rest of her life: balk at buttonholes, sigh at Christmas wreaths, reject a wedding bouquet.

'What's the matter with you?' the wedding planner will say.

★

The horticulturist appreciated his asthma. It got him out of gym class; he wielded his inhaler like a wand. The pretty girl he dated in high school called him her wounded prince, then left him, a little bored by his lack of athleticism. Sometimes she ran through his mind on a hot Wednesday afternoon.

He lost his job with the Parks department because of his chest; his wife said he needed patience. So he sold cigarettes some days, three for a buck, and stepped patiently between two young bloods fighting over a pretty woman on the street.

They're slow to stop; their angry cries shatter the concrete. The policemen who come are fools, and the chokehold that brings the horticulturist down is more illegal than cigarettes.

*I have asthma*, thought the horticulturist. *Don't you know?*

★

Phyllis Wilson went to the store to buy bread. When she got back with a Battenburg cake and a hot saveloy from the chippy, her sixteen-year-old son was lying handcuffed on her living room floor, with his cheek against the TV Guide.

Sleeping, Phyllis thought, stepping in and contemplating her son's other cheek, sitting across the way on her clean kitchen table.

The police buzz around her apartment, apologising.

★

Imagine, dem jus' kill di gyal fi no good reason. Say dem *t'ink* she know one a dem gunman who operate through Port Antonio. All di gyal do is stand up deh next to di gunman bwoy and police come open fire pon di two a dem like she name calataral damage.

Miss Doris down di road tell mi seh dem couldn't see neider of dem face after corpie done. Bradap-brap-brap-brrrrrrr. You know 'bout M16.

★

My father believed in Heaven all my life.

Every Sunday, in church. Hands up in the air: amazing grace.
At the funeral.
Here to tell you there ain't no Heaven, Papa.
Ain't no Heaven here.

*RIP Tamir Rice, Sheku Bayoh, Joy Gardner, Michael Brown, John Charles de Menezes, Eric Garner, Walter Scott, Kajieme Powell, Kimani Gray, Phillip White, Kendrec McDade, Amadou Diallo, Patrick Dorismond, Ousmane Zongo, Timothy Stansbury, Sandra Bland, Sean Bell, Korryn Gaines, Orlando Barlow, John Crawford III, Aaron Campbell, Sarah Reed, Victor Steen, Tanisha Anderson, Freddie Gray, Alonzo Ashley. And those to come.*

## ROLL IT

The woman has fifteen minutes before she dies on the catwalk.

She stands behind the cheap black curtain that separates backstage from runway, peeping out at the audience as they clap and su-su behind their hands. It's so dark. The open-air runway loops through the botanical garden and the murmuring specta-tors. No one in Jamaica has seen a fashion show like this before. Strobe lights and naked torches blend, mottling the faces of the barefooted models as they negotiate hundreds of golden candles scattered across the stage.

They are all dressed as monsters.

A hot gust of wind bursts through the palms and banana trees, pushing against the curtain where the woman is waiting to die. She watches as one of the other models stumbles, steps on a candle and stretches her long neck up to the sky – a wordless screaming, like eating the air. The audience laugh and gasp and admire the vivid blue dress clinging to her body and the thick fake blood on her arms and clumped in her long, processed hair. She is dressed as a vampire, what country people call Old Higue.

★

'Gimme more blood, nuh.' That was what Parker said at rehearsal last week. He was surprised when the stage manager explained it was vegetable dye.

'So where is the artistic integrity?'

Parker: her husband. Not handsome. His father broke his nose before he was fourteen and it always seemed on the brink of splintering again. At school they'd called him a batty-man and so his eyes are watchful.

He walked over to her and bent down so close his eyelashes touched her cheek, ignoring the jealous glances around them.

'You alright, baby? When we go home, I rub your… feet.'

The woman moaned quietly against his shoulder. The other models thought of his voice poured over their wrists; of adjusted hems and skilfully placed pins and the hold-breath moment when his quick fingers brushed their bare skin.

Parker laughed and turned from her, whirling to face the rest of them, fierce and happy.

'You are *all* my beautiful ghosts!'

★

Fourteen minutes: the woman sweats. Behind her and the black curtain, a white passage looms, ending in a makeshift tent, where the models change. Girls run to and fro, on and off stage, or stand and wait, like her. She can hear the clapping each time the curtain rises, like the ticking of a clock. It is midsummer and Kingston seems hotter than ever; the whirring upright fans around her only stir the heavy air. Sweat trickles down her neck-back and between her thighs. Moisture beads on her top lip. She's used to being the hottest person in the room. She hopes her make-up won't run. At home she cranks the air conditioning high until Parker arrives. She always slips a hand-fan in her purse for the walk between the car park and the supermarket.

The waiting girls sigh and murmur, strung along the passage, cutting shadowed eyes at her. She's used to the way their dangling thighs and backbones remind her of an abattoir. She's seen many of them come and go through the years, so beautiful, but never friendly. Chandelier silver earrings tangle in shop-bought hair; heavy golden creole earrings pull at piercings, fall and are scooped up again, tsk-ing irritation; bells and beads tinkle and clack;

jerked-straight hems and wrists and feathered details; crochet and hand embroidery.

'Anybody have a nail clipper?' The girl asking looks anxious. Parker doesn't allow long fingernails.

The woman waiting to die watches as the girls climb the six steps up to the stage; disappear through the curtain slit and return minutes later, triumphant. Some pant and pump the air with their fists, others are silent and professional; they dash back up the passage and into the tent for the next costume.

She will only walk this one dress tonight.

Thirteen minutes. Maybe twelve, now.

Two whispering women slink past.

'She get di best dress again?'

'Weh yuh expec'?'

Years of people saying things so faraway and low that she shouldn't be able to hear, but does. The sweat prickles. She pulls the soft fabric away from her chest, blows down her cleavage gently, rocking. Another girl comes back through the curtain; her transparent black lace dress exposes flat, dark breasts and a g-string that is scarlet and wet, like a wound. Red contact lenses, flaming red wig. In the countryside, the old men who work as ghost hunters give girls red underwear to fend off the succubus at night.

The woman shudders.

'Move, nuh,' says the red girl and runs up the passage.

The hot woman watches her go, then turns back to the curtain.

★

Before he began to sketch and cut and sew, Parker gave the models ghost stories to read.

'This is not just some duppy story. I want you to *embody* them.'

One girl looked confused. Later, the woman took her aside to explain what 'embody' meant.

★

Twelve, oh twelve minutes. She could sing eleven. The air stinks of the blood Parker mixed in with the vegetable dye and body paint. Each time a girl slithers through the curtain, the woman thinks of a goat giving birth, legs first, a glut of liquid.

Slip in, slip out.

The albino girl up next is new. She wears a cream wedding dress the exact colour of her skin and a tattered veil over the yellow dreadlocks weaved into her yellow hair. Hundreds of cream silk roses fall from the bodice, pour down her back and weep into the ground. Parker heard the gossips talking about her: a tall *dundus* girl, living near Matilda's Corner. He paraded her through their living room, with her hair the colour of straw and her golden eyes. He waved the book of ghost stories.

'Now *that* is my White Witch of Rose Hall!' Later he told the woman how angry he was about the way the dundus was treated.

'Ignorant rassclaat dem. You can call a girl like that ugly?'

★

The woman watches the dundus and her wide, nervous eyes and thinks of the legend of the White Witch – a young English bride, brought over to the Rose Hall slave plantation to live like a queen. She had children whipped in the front yard of her great-house and disembowelled one of her maids just after breakfast. When the slaves rose to kill her, her ghost returned to slaughter them in their dreams.

What could have made her cruel, so?

The dundus hoists herself up the steps, two-three, another girl lifting the bans o' roses train so she doesn't trip.

★

Parker was happy when things went to plan. Sometimes when he was happy and sleeping, she slipped out and walked the cooling Kingston roads, too late even for gunman. Found her way in pitch blackness; she'd never needed lamp or torch. The occasional driver caught her in the headlights, whizzed past her, open-mouthed.

When she was tired, she clanked home.

★

'Aaaah,' say the fashionista crowd, out under the stars and the green expanse of Hope Gardens.

★

She came here for the first time as a girl – on a school trip to the funfair, where there were American things like bumper cars and whirl-a-gigs and a train, and the older girls laughed at her barely-hidden delight. They would rather be in the plaza, eating banana chips and what you wearing to the party up Norbrook tonight, who driving? But she remembered the whoosh and creak of the rides and the pink bouffant candyfloss. It all seemed magical, this fairground in the middle of a place called Hope.

Nine minutes: who can she say these things to?

★

Parker found her sitting under a poui tree, far away from the funfair when the teasing from the other girls got bad. Fifteen years old, long bare legs and trying to do her homework. She was already a year behind, 'sake of stupid, her mother said, and how she couldn't bother beat her anymore, because if you beat even a mule too much, it back bow and the only chance she had for a life was her looks. Even though men said she was too maaga and tall, and what a way she *black*, they liked her oval face and the way she moved down the street.

The woman didn't care what she looked like, because what she really wanted more than anything else was to get three A's and go to the law school at UWI. She'd been up there to watch the student mock trials and the black robes. But every day she picked up her books, the letters jittered like Kumina dancers and slid away – now why did that B have to move its way back behind the H? It was the misbehaving letters standing between she and UWI and a chance to come and sit here in Hope Gardens and read law books. Her mother said she was lazy but it wasn't true. Eventually she'd put on a black robe and say, I'm a lawyer, Mama, and what you think about that?

One day, her mother would burn.

Parker saved her.

★

She must walk well in eight minutes. She still rolls her hips; all Jamaican models do. It is something they hear when they go abroad. You have to walk runway with your legs and shoulders; only Naomi Campbell can get away with a hip-sway, and everyone knows she's old-school anyway. Once, in New York, a stage manager screamed at her.

'I told you not to walk like a whore, bitch! How many *times*?'

She thinks that Parker is a visionary. That is what they call him in the newspapers. But so many people here misunderstand him. They say he's weird and wacky and that the heavy jewellery he wears would look better on a woman.

People are stupid.

★

'I going make you famous, sweet gyal,' Parker said, under the poui tree. At her first runway show he dressed them all in exquisitely tailored black dresses and masks like fly eyes and gave them small, sharp machetes to carry. He said they were mosquitos, the kind that gave you dengue fever.

She understood his concept immediately.

'Walk like your back is broken,' he said. 'You know how mosquitos crouch on your arm before they bite you? He made a claw with his hand to demonstrate.

She wasn't thinking much when she corrected him:

'Mosquitos don't bite, they push in a tube thing'. She was too busy struggling to remember the word proboscis, which was one of those words that danced across the page and slipped off into the grass, when his backhand pitched her over a table. She landed before she had a chance to think about falling and lay bent at three different angles, too incredulous to be frightened. Here was a P by her throbbing head and there a golden R by her broken fingernail – 'I never tell you, cut your nails?' And she thought: *You lie, no, is not so it go. He never just. He never.*

And the jealous eyes.

'Him beat her because him love her.'

Was that true?

Picked her, sweating in Hope Gardens, like a poui blossom.

★

Seconds are long, bare things. She experiences them as if she is walking through a rainforest, thin green branches sticking into her flesh. She shifts her bare feet, catches the eye of another girl waiting to go onstage. The girl smiles, sharp incisors poking over her lips. She is a river mumma, her dress made of silver-green fish scales, but she is also like fruit, a knobbled soursop.

'Smile. Let them see your teeth,' Parker had instructed. 'And when you reach the front, cry. A river mumma is a wet thing.'

The woman wonders whether the girl will bring it off.

★

She recalls her mother telling her duppy stories at night, she face down in her bed, the weals on her back and shoulders too fresh to lie any other way: stories about the man who picked up a stranger in his car and the stranger had long, jagged teeth and the driver jumped out of his car and ran and ran and ran, gasping, sweating, begging shelter from a woman fishing by the riverbank.

'Lady, help me, I just pick up a duppy wid long teeth,' and the river mumma turned around and smiled.

'Teeth like these?'

★

Even the most ignorant people can *read* the ingredients on a box juice and the words on a billboard and she likes watching matinees on Sunday television because she doesn't have to *read*, although Parker's mother likes foreign movies with subtitles and when they visit she's glad she's already picked up a little *parley vous Francais* on her travels and can say something when Parker's mother asks her what she thinks about the movie.

The dundus girl comes back through the curtain in her wedding dress, happy face like a peeled egg. She can rest now; there's no other work for her tonight and the woman wonders: Now that she's been Parker's White Witch, will she ever get work again? She watches the yellow girl walk away, sees her reach down and pluck one of the raw silk roses from the train and slip it in her mouth. They are so succulent; no wonder she's moved to stealing. She has stood at her own front door, dressed in Parker's beautiful clothing, which is always so light and expensive, and underneath the trappings of his imagination, so kind to a woman's body. Has felt the maid passing, sweeping, admiring.

'You going out, Miss…?'

'No.'

Nobody remembers her *name*: has no one at the *Gleaner* or the *Observer* or on JMTV ever noticed that?

'Parker James' favourite model…'

'Parker James' model wife considers retirement at 30…'

The woman leans towards the river mumma, who leans towards her as the seconds thunder past and the chains around her bare feet crackle. Parker says the chains have to be heavy.

More than anything else, she knows he will never change.

'What is my name?' she asks.

River mumma frowns. 'How you mean?'

*

She remembers Parker sitting beside her, under the poui tree, picking up her History book. He had the right kind of voice for bedtime stories. He read the first page and the second, and the third, and she found herself melting against the tree trunk. She could hardly breathe, his voice was so pretty. He still reads to her at night, fifteen years later, everything she's ever loved: Shakespeare and Jean Binta Breeze and Naipaul and Dickens. She can lean back and lose herself in different worlds, his voice deep and sure, his hands on her waist afterwards, so gentle, hissing into her neck:

'You hot inside, sweet gyal.'

She used to hope that someone else would come along one day and read her stories. But she knew it wouldn't happen. No one would sound like him and she didn't have to fill in her name on the forms at the hospital because everyone there knew who she was.

*

She brushes her hand up and down her body; the chains jingle and she tells herself it is just like jewellery. Parker usually hides the damage in her scalp, in the cleft of her buttocks and between her thighs, but finally he can be gleeful and unrestrained. The bruises are purple and yellow and black; fist-sized lumps across her shoulders. There is a bruise on the sole of her left foot.

All for his artistic integrity.

Four minutes. River mumma is finishing her circuit – the woman knows by the rising claps. Has she cried enough to please Parker? He is waiting in the front row, at the foot of the stage.

She always walks ramp as his last model, the best in show. He will mount the stage to hold her hand and take the final bow.

'Perfect,' he said, when the make-up artist brought the old chains to loop around her feet and throat. His fingers trembled as he dressed and turned her, so she could see herself in the full-length mirror. His eyes were wet.

'Did I make you beautiful?'

His needy fingers on her concave belly.

'Oh, yes.'

She can't leave this love. And Parker will be what he is, forever.

The woman who is about to die remembers her mother's stories.

'You can hear it?'

She reaches up, mimics her mother, cupping her ear.

'Listen good: rolling calf a-walk.'

She has always felt the power of the legend of the rolling calf. There are so few details, as if people have been struck dumb with the terror, but they say your head swells and lifts before the rolling calf comes in the night; that you can feel your feet rising from the floor. Clanking chain and hoarse panting in the distance. Is that a roar outside? Hooves clitter-clatter, clunk. Hiss of fire, smell of smoke. Never, ever-ever look into its burning orange eyes, and if you hear it coming, curse bad words! Curse as loud and long as you can and pray the rolling calf go on past your house. It can bruise you with its flailing chain, even with its back turned. Flame eyes, dragging broken chain, ripped free… from what?

Hell, hell. She knows.

She climbs the steps and parts the curtains: *Aaaah*, say the audience.

Flame creeps up the cheap black fabric where her fingers cling. The orange dress he made especially for her crackles on her skin; her nostrils flare at the smell of ash. The chains are hot and violent snakes, surging down her thighs. Her belly is suffused in golden fire. She laughs at the candles. Thrusts her hand into a naked torch, up to the armpit; there is no pain anymore.

People scream and clutch their heads; scatter and pray. A few curse rich and juicy epithets through the dark night air. Others float, inches from the steaming grass. She can hear Parker, screaming at the end of the catwalk. Screaming for his precious dress.

'No, no, *no*!'

*Whoomph!* Her hair burns. Her bruises peel away under the heat, like black paper.

*Roll your hips*, she thinks.

Her eyes burn last.

## DRAG

Today I feel like a drag queen. Walking down Soho way through the tourists and the catcalls. My crotch is aching under the good jeans and the bad underwear, watching the freaks go by, acres of eyeliner and jangly earrings and crap t-shirts that pass for fashion, walking and making sure my hips sway in calypso circles.

Today I feel like a drag queen. The top layer of me is a bouncin' an' behavin' woman; I'm all rounded tits and a belly button so deep you could play strip poker inside it. But I feel like a boy. Eighteen years old, slim hips, shoulders so strong I could carry the world, baby-soft face and mascara eyes. The boy in me lengthens my stride and gives me attitude. He looks out from under my eyelashes. I'm working it. I'm being seen. I'm shimmying.

'The only thing I want to drink more than a beer tonight is you.'

I look up. He's not my type. His head would bang into doorways. We couldn't dance; I'd be stuck just above his navel. I don't like liquorice-flavoured men. But today the boy inside me needs a fuck. From any body. He's leaning against a porn shop; it's the days when people still used them. I can see those plastic ribbon thingies they insist you pass through, like a time machine. I think that his face is open, that it reminds me of a child's. He is even yummy, with a second glance.

I look at him. Grin.

'Going inside?' I ask.

'No.'

He laughs.

'Come inside with me.'

We wander around the interior. It's dark and silly and small waves of embarrassed men part before us. They pretend none of us are there. I pick up the worst of the porn, speak loudly, point out cum shots and women dressed as little girls. I even find a puzzled, swollen donkey. We discuss dick sizes at the tops of our voices, pretending to be serious. Men begin to leave. The proprietor looks indignant. I turn more pages, laugh and watch our arms, side by side, nearly identical shades of dark. His soft lips thrust through stubble.

'What's your name?' he asks.

'Jo.' I test the diminutive on my tongue. He looks amused. As if he understands my gender shenanigans just fine.

'Joanna? Josephine?'

'Just Jo, call me Jo.'

'I'm Michael,' he says. I like the way he says his name. Like it fits him, like he's new. Like he's the only Michael in the world. The proprietor grimaces and rolls his eyes. We are nearly alone in the shop. The last man is trying not to look me in the face as he wriggles past us. He wants to fuck me, but he doesn't want me to see that. Michael moves to let him go by. I love that he doesn't try to protect me. He stands next to me, trusting me in my own space, like I'm his equal. Like I'm strong.

★

Back at my flat he lays me across my bed, in between pages of my thesis. I am writing about black people in 80s British ads – like how there were none. He doesn't care. The head of his dick is swollen and purple-red. He is watching me closely. I tighten the muscles in my stomach, flex my shoulders. I want my body to feel like concrete. I run my hands along my thighs, pretending the hair there is pepper-grains. I'm holding the bunch of roses he bought me in Leicester Square. A thorn sticks through my flesh and I can feel blood on my palm.

Michael crouches over me and pulls the roses away slowly. Then he is ripping them apart and scattering petals, stalks, thorns, across my breasts.

'Tell me how you want me to be,' he pants.

'Fuck me like I'm a boy,' I say.

He puts a thumb up my cunt, parting the folds. A small sword through honey. I twist away, annoyed. 'No,' I say. My voice is shaking, I want him to understand so bad, but I don't want to talk. 'Like you're fucking yourself.'

He's lying on top of me, his cock rubbing against my tummy. It's wet there. He rubs himself across me, hipbone to hipbone. He's running a bass line through me; I can feel it everywhere. He licks the blood off my palm, thoughtfully.

'That's hardly safe,' I say.

'So?' he says, and flips me over. My clit's rubbing against the white duvet and I can imagine it growing, swelling, tumescent, hard against my belly. He's spitting on his fingers, rubbing them up and down my asshole. His breath is lost in my hair. He pauses against the entrance, like there's a stop sign. Like he needs permission just one more time.

'Go on,' I say. I've never done this before and it needs to be now.

He pushes gently. The head slips in. Agony. I twist, trying to accommodate.

'Oh fuck,' he groans against my ear.

I feel like a girl, about to be taken; I fight against the femininity. I don't want it, not today. I want the abandonment, the urgency of a boy, but it's no good. I'm afraid. Straining, anxious, I push myself onto my elbows. He's still being tentative, he's halfway in, but my body is groaning, rejecting it. He's sliding into a tube of sandpaper. My whole body is shaking, my head is shaking. Maybe I'm not a boy. A million pins dance the length of my ass.

'Michael, let's stop –'

He ignores me, thrusts a hand underneath us, begins to play with my clit, twisting, insistent, rubbing me in hard circles. I love the weight of him on top of me. I am pinned in a slow-moving dream.

'No…' I say, but it's working. I can feel my ass melting, widening, moisture seeping.

'Your name is Michael.' He whispers it against my hair. 'It's Carnival. You're up against a brick wall, and I'm fucking you in the ass. Your cock is rubbing against the wall. You're so hard. We met five minutes ago.'

He's all the way inside me, a metal bar against my ass cheeks, the heel of his hand grinding into my clit, and nothing hurts anymore. I can hear myself. I'm growling and I can hear the soca in the distance and when I look up I can see shocked grannies, amused revellers. I can see a policeman cocking his head to the side: *Are they really doing that?* He starts up the street, ready to arrest two queer niggers.

I have no breasts. My chest is flat. I shift, undulate. I've become a smooth runway that pours from the base of my arched neck, down my shoulder blades, spreads around my hips, pushes me up and into him. I'm gleaming with afternoon sweat. Michael takes a breath, pulls half way out, plunges into me, vicious.

I howl. Delicious.

Afterwards, he knows how to be. I tell him my full, girl name.

★

Today I feel like an executive. My hair is scraped off my face and the make-up is flawless. Walking into a classy restaurant, the London sun streams through the French windows, melting the clientele like individual ice cream cakes. I'm wearing a black suit and peach lingerie. My heels are sensible and expensive. Before I leave the office my boss tells me to use everything I've got. He winks. He thinks he's a feminist. But he is not above pimping me out.

Today I feel like an executive. Facts and figures flow from my fingertips. I am articulate and assertive. But underneath is so much more: an ambitious twenty-five year-old who lies in the bath and dreams of power. Rubber duck in the bath tells me I should have a flat on the Riviera, a penthouse in New York. Bubbles promise me a walk-in closet of designer clothes, three personal assistants and gleaming, lavish technology. I am a multi-million deal.

'Josephine…' I love his voice. I look up. He's in a sharp, dark suit, impeccably tailored. Women's heads swivel. *Blond bitches*, I think, and clutch my glass of water. He scoops condensation from the edge and rubs it between his fingers. I can't stop looking. I remember his hands on me.

'Long time no see,' I say.

'So?' he says. Climbs right in next to me.

'You can't stay.' My thighs are humming. 'I have a business meeting.'

He introduces himself as my colleague when the client arrives. The client orders tea and discusses cost-effectiveness, the implications of visual versus voice-over, whether we need a celebrity or normal actresses. He says there are other ad companies waiting in line. I nod and sound intelligent. Michael puts his hand up my skirt. My knees snap together. He is cupping me, like I'm an exquisite thing. I can smell myself: pussy mixed with golden lilies at the windowsill.

He uses one long, insistent finger. Rubs just above my clitoris. I twitch, trying to edge him nearer the brink of me. Inside I'm an empty roll of wet muscles. I could play him like a flute, if only we were far from here. Another finger strokes my pubic hair. I wonder if the teasing is hesitance or deliberate, then suck in my breath as he hits the mark, just to show off. Deliberate, then. Back to the top. Then down again. Almost imperceptible circles. I try to slow my breathing.

'You see, we think that speaking to women in their own language will knock the socks off the competition,' says the client. A single crumb sits on his neat moustache. I want to lick it off. I want to grab his head and push it between my breasts and scream. I want them both to fuck me across the table.

'…perhaps animation…' says the client.

'Mmm-hmmm,' I say.

Michael's finger eases inside me, taking all the daylight in the room with it. I am sitting in a pool of summer. He puts a thumb back on my clit and it jumps up like its Christmas. I push my hips forward. Tiny, tight, urgent, circles.

'Could you, um, order some coffee?' I say to the client.

He turns and signals for the waitress. Michael pulls his hand out of me and licks his fingers. One. Two. Three. I hide a groan in my napkin. The client turns back and smiles at me, clueless. My lips are stuck to my teeth. Michael asks him a question. I can't hear him. I've gone deaf. The client leans forward. Michael leans towards him so he can put his fingers back under the table, twiddling me, all in one motion. I sip scalding coffee. Burn my tongue. Put my hand on top of Michael's hand. Press him into me.

'Harder...' I say.

'Pardon?' says the client.

'It must be hard to... deal with established competitors. It must get harder every day. Harder and *harder*.'

'Ah,' says the client.

I want to close my eyes. I can feel my orgasm tickling the base of my spine. I'm talking and talking and the words are scrabble squares on a board: meaningless, but full of potential. I want to lean back in my chair. Tell them both that one day I'll be able to buy them with a flick of my well-manicured hands. Michael puts his hand on my inner thigh and pushes my legs as wide as they can go. Grasps my panties and pushes them roughly aside. I can hear a rip. He pushes something small and cold up me. My hand on the table goes into involuntary spasm. Michael makes me touch myself with my other hand. Neither of us have taken our eyes off the chattering client; thank God he is the pontificating kind. Michael bites his bottom lip as our entwined fingers touch the tiny globes he's pushed inside me. They feel as if they should be silver. We stir them around. My hand is frothy. They tinkle, I'm sure. The client is talking. Michael leans into my shoulder.

'Do it,' he says.

My hips buck. I'm beyond speech. All I can do is breathe with the waves. My breasts are spilling out of my bra, they're so swollen. He's rubbing my clit the way I like it, hard and God, so dirty, and the balls are revolving, tinkling, pulling it all out of me. I surrender, lean forward into the table cloth.

'Are you alright?' the men chorus above me. The client is calling, 'Waitress, Waitress, she's having a fit.' Everybody around me is looking afraid and concerned: 'Is she choking? Someone do the Heimlich thingie' and Michael is all the way up in my face, one arm round my shoulder. 'Jo, you ok? Say something,' but there's a twinkle in his eye and I can tell what he's thinking: *Be quick, Josephine, be cost effective, cum for me, before the place erupts. I'm going to have to take my hand away. Cum for me* and then I'm screaming. I can't believe I'm doing it. There's something so powerful about it all. I'm cumming *in their faces* and nobody knows, my nails are scraping the tablecloth and someone cries out as the coffee cup shatters on the floor and I'm trying not to laugh, my cute little ass still jerking, thank Christ for that thick table-cloth, you know those slow wave, post-cum jerks that feel like aftershocks and I've put my fingernails through the flesh between Michael's neck and his shoulder and I can tell it really hurts him, but he's trying not to laugh, and even as the waitress rushes over he coaxes out another tiny, extra orgasm, 'cause he's greedy like that, and then it's done and he's wiping his hand all over his face, so cool, like all he's been is stressed for my health and I'm like *fuck, fuck,* I want to laugh, that's all I feel like doing: laughing.

So I do. Delicious.

Afterwards the client rings to make sure I'm alright.

We get the deal.

★

Today I feel like a bride. Pacing the special room set aside for me at the back of the church. All Vera Wang class. If I could blush I'd be doing that in the mirror. There's an hour to go. My bridesmaids – all ten of them – have floated away, leaving 'me time'. I don't know where they came from. None of them are my friends.

My dress has cost twelve thousand pounds. Freshwater pearls at the hemline and the bodice. Diamonds snigger in my ear and make promises. The dress reminds me of Victoria Falls at sunset, a huge flow of everything white in the world: roaring snowflakes, pools of chalk dust, bleached frost.

Today I feel like a bride. Fragrant. I am every love song ever played. I am pink confetti. I am the wedding march personified. I am God's best promise, an open sack, waiting to be filled with matrimonially blessed seed. I am hope. But underneath I am a thirty-five year-old woman who is slipping, gratefully, off the shelf. A wedding cake, blind drunk with brandy. I am the solemn, desperate hopes of my mother. I have lost my way. I have no choice.

'You're beautiful.' I look up. I don't know how he got in. He's older and it looks so good on him.

'Thank you,' I say.

'So…' Michael says. He sits down at my feet, cross-legged. I can barely see him over the lace.

'What?' I say. 'What do you *want*?'

He shakes his head. Unfolds himself, tall. Then he is back, with a small blue bowl. I can smell the lotion: it's my grand-mother's kitchen.

'What is it?' I say.

'I made it.'

He takes one perfect shoe off my foot. His hands are warm in the breeze dancing through the open church. His palms are tender, and my body is already sweeter than it was before, like someone dropped sugarcane into my heart, pumped it through my bloodstream. He traces patterns on my soles, my ankles, my thighs, pushing up through miles of dress. I sit down, legs wide, my back against the wall. I am whimpering as he runs his soft tongue through the hair down there, plaiting me, dipping his tongue into me. His moistened hands have slipped under the dress's bodice, and my breasts feel young again. Perky, coffee-coloured beginnings. My nipples are tiny silver balls.

He is rubbing his magic lotion into my crotch, pouring it across my thighs. It drips off my soft belly, puddles and sinks into twelve thousand pounds worth of promises. He parts the lips of my pussy, as if in prayer. I watch him rubbing warm lotion over his cock, one hand on my hip. Then there are careful inches, pushing inside me.

I groan.

We have never made love before. I wonder why as I gather him into me. I wonder why, because this is a symphony of scent and breath, high notes of lemon and the pure sob of cinnamon and the darkness of cloves. I wonder why as I say his name, over and over, like I'm hushing a baby. It is almost too good.

His hand dives between our bodies. I listen to the old, familiar sound of him rubbing me. His eyes are kind as I gasp and drum my fists against his back.

'So this is what you feel like…' he says. He's trying to be cool, but his voice is too shaky. I smile, my eyes closed.

'Does it feel good?' I want him to feel good.

'Oh yes,' he says, and pushes his hips forward once more. His penis is kissing me, tiny wet kisses along the length of me, so certain. He looks into my face. One finger, delicate, gathers the tear on my cheek.

'Who am I?' I say.

Michael pushes into me and reminds me who I am. He tears off one pearl and fucks me juicy. He tears another and fucks me deep. I join him, fingernails sliding through cloth and lace. The dress disintegrates, baring me dark and sticky against the church floor. I'm throwing pearls across the room. We sound like animals, coughing primal sounds over our lips and chins. My hands are digging into his ass, pushing him further in. I have a finger inside him where it's hot and secret, guiding him, showing him how to move. He is whining, but through it all saying: 'Who are you, who are you, who *are* you?' And I'm a drag queen, eighteen years old, trying a little something-something with the new beat of my clit; I'm a twenty-five-year-old executive – even though I never made a million; I'm years of expectations; I'm a cop-out, thinking I needed to be Cinderella cause God knows my mother needs grandchildren. I'm a fuck, I'm a friend, yeah

I remember who they are. I'm enough, I'm enough, I'm just right.

Birds whistle at the window.

Afterwards, I leave him in a pile. Run down the aisle, cupping what's left of Vera Wang to my tits, the wedding party's mouths slack with shock, but I can see delight in a few who are glad. Out into the shuddering afternoon light. I hail a cab. Kick my bare feet up on the glass between me, and the man at the wheel.

Delicious.

'Drive,' I say.

## BREAKFAST TIME

Tina wakes up at 6.30 a.m and takes out the earplugs. Pink carnations rustle at the window; someone has forgotten to close it and cold air loops through. She reaches up to tuck the urine-coloured blanket around her left shoulder. Everything hurts. Hospital wards are noisy, especially at night. The nurses try to speak in low voices but low voices are unnatural and so they succumb to both failure and impatience.

The old woman lying in the bed next to her is called Rose and specialises in theatrical complaint. She forgets she can shit where she lies, into a special bag made for that purpose, so she yells for a nurse whenever she feels the urge, even at 2 a.m. Tina hates Rose and wishes she would die. Tina presses the call button when she needs a nurse and when they come at night she keeps her voice down.

A man yells in the ward next door: he sounds drunk. A nurse speaks to him. She sounds professional, like someone slipped razor blades into her voice. The man calls her a nurse cunt. There is a bang and a squawk. Tina's eyes widen. A male nurse runs up the hallway and there are scuffling sounds. Rose sleeps on, her toothless mouth moving. Nothing disturbs *her*.

The scuffles die down. The drunk man is promising to behave, only that it huuurts, it huuurts.

Tina watches Rose smile in her sleep. Rose might have no teeth, but when the physiotherapists walk her around the ward in the morning, her back is straight, toes turned out, her smile imperious.

Tina reaches down for her stitches; she'll look like that soon. Curved and carved and perfect.

She smiles.

Belly. It has not cost her lovers or work. She confounds men and theatre critics, which is to say she confounds most men. She's made it her mission to distract them from her imperfection, and so critics speak of her unexpected Desdemona and the soaring energy of her Abigail Williams and lovers handle her body with suspicion and awe and casual words:

'You are quite beautiful, you know. And onstage… yes.'

What they mean is fat and what they mean is that they cannot forget the fat and what they mean is that they enjoyed her despite the fat.

The fat will be gone soon.

The ward stirs. Breakfast is imminent. A nurse says good morning and asks if Tina needs pain relief. Yes. Morphine, as always. She likes it. It is a pretty, smooth high and all she needs to do for more is demand it. She rolls over and the nurse points the needle at the big muscle in her rear, below the hip.

'A sharp scratch,' she warns.

Tina wriggles her toes as the needle goes in, then presses and rubs the sting. She remembers the first morphine, the day after surgery. Blurred eyes, lying giggling, looking at the three other women in the ward alongside her, morphed into strange objects. A huge peach pit. A crumpled piece of newspaper. Rose was a lobster shell. Tina lay for an hour, looking at them, singing under her breath as they slowly changed back into themselves.

Above the bed, she is named and defined: Tina Bernard. Nil by mouth. Her mouth is dry. She's not eaten for two days and is conscious of the cannula in the back of her left hand, its plastic needle buried into the vein, lacing away from her towards a beeping machine. The drip makes her feel like a real patient, like people in hospital TV shows. She has to take it to the bathroom with her, rolling it across the floor, tucking it in beside her as she lowers haunches to the toilet. The cannula doesn't hurt, but it's alien and she fears her sleeping movements will dislodge it. It only lasts a day at a time, any longer and her wrist balloons, then hurts, her body rejecting the invader. Nurses move over her, tutting and comforting, to remove it. 'My, you're sensitive,' one says. But she likes the cannula. The saline feels cold and thin in her veins and it makes her pee in waterfalls.

She snakes her right hand down her swollen abdomen again. The surgeon says there will be minimal scarring and that makes her want to laugh, and then to hide, thinking of him poring over her belly, snipping and tying off – whatever surgeons do. He will have seen that one more scar will make no difference, lost between the stretch marks, ripples and bulges. She remembers the face of the GP who suggested bariatric surgery, how angry she was, and the righteousness of her girlfriends – how dare he, she must report him for insensitivity, for political incorrectness, for something.

Then, a month ago, lying in a deep bath, she had regarded the belly. She's spent years pretending it isn't there. Has learned how to dress, to make love, to dance, to take the stage in ways that hide it from herself. But now she sees it, curving above the water, a bulbous, horrid thing. She closes her eyes and tries to make it beautiful: apricot-coloured, glowing in the light.

Such a spell is not possible.

She has done this alone. No one knows she is here.

★

She dozes. The ward lights brighten and nurses bustle. Breakfast is served at 7.30 a.m. to the patients who aren't nil by mouth. The orderlies wheel the food trolley past her, yelling at the old women stirring:

'Cereal, Mrs. Brown. Do you want cereal? Cornflakes? Porridge? Tea, Mrs. Brown? No, *tea*! Do you want tea?'

It has been splendid to fast, to feed on salt water and morphine. Starvation is a revelation; when they eventually come to her with food she fears she'll scream. She doesn't want them adding psychological problems to her chart. She reads the chart to see what they say about her. Patient is independent. Patient asked for pain relief. Patient read for several hours and slept well. She's been a good girl. She doesn't want a bad report card.

This is a new life. She can be a sculpture. They've clamped her inside. Two ounces, they say. That's all you'll hold. She imagines days of choosing carefully: beautifully whipped mashed potatoes, one spoon, two spoons, done; a celery stick that fills her up; a meal of freshly squeezed orange juice.

A nurse pats the blankets around her and says her name. She unscrews the looping, plastic drip. The beep cuts out, like someone died.

'I have a surprise for you,' says the nurse. 'Today you get breakfast. Won't that be nice? Then you can have a nice wash and a walk, eh?'

★

It has been twelve days. Tina disturbs the patients at night; she can't stop crying. The nurses are worried and they speak to her at all hours, matter-of-fact, or sweet as lilies, or like razor blades or ticking watches: nothing changes. There is talk of moving her somewhere else.

She can't eat because the food is talking to her. Her first spoon of clear soup chattered down her throat, commenting on the architecture – panelling, refurbishment, ceiling structure. When she swallowed, puzzled, the voice stuttered, like a damaged old CD disc. The single teaspoon of broth kept on chatting inside her tiny stomach – she could hear it, half a second behind the voice in the cup before her – an irritating, doubling effect that made her head swim. She vomited then, weak and surprised.

The nurses say the nausea is usual and she shouldn't worry, but she does. The segmented clementine on Rose's table hums a reggae song. The raspberry jam on other people's toast laughs at her as it disappears down ill and wrinkled throats. She tries to tell the doctors that something's changed, but they look at charts and they look through her and they tell her about case studies.

'Calm down,' one says. She is Roman-nosed and looks as if she's smelled something bad.

★

Tina stares at a quarter of a mashed banana on the tray before her. She's hungry, but the banana is reciting the Spanish alphabet in patient, liquid tones. The spoon beside it begins to vibrate.

'Comrades!'

A cup across the room: 'Comrade?'

'Welcome to our third Annual General Meeting, Comrades! Join me while we sing! Arise, ye soldiers of all nations...'

'Condemned to misery and woe!'

'To hell with humbleness and patience!'

'Give deadly battle to the foe!'

Their voices rise shrilly. The fork beats time. A pat of butter purrs. The mashed banana begins the nine-times table. A breadcrumb squeaks. Rose stares at her, mouth slack, raspberry jam dripping down her chin.

Tina is screaming.

She is losing weight.

## PALS

they said she needed a head but she was quite fine without one not knowing any different and the kids at school got used to it once they'd had Mrs Jenkins in from disability services some people said it was the missing eyes that troubled them the most but her best friend Alison said people didn't look into your eyes anyway and so that was bollocks describe me she once said to Alison when they were fifteen and she felt different and bad and didn't want to take her dog Trapeze everywhere because people didn't know you weren't supposed to play with him and she was worried she smelled of dog

your collarbones are shiny said Alison and your shoulders are nice and strong and instead of shaking your head you shake your hips plus you've got better tits than me so you'll be fine really? she said oh don't be silly said Alison no dandruff no eyelash tinting or face waxing no rouge no sloppy kissing no fags and more space in your handbag coz you don't need lippy no headaches here put these heels on now you're ready for a boogie the girl with no head clapped her hands instead of smiling only try not to do that thing when your heart pops through the top of your neck because that does put people off why? she said well it swells up when you're excited and you don't want Billy Jenners knowing you like him do you?

## PRESIDENT DAISY

Mary sat on the train and worried about it going bang-a-lang underneath her. Her cousin Toby said that when the train started up it would make bang-a-lang noises because it was full of devils trying to get out. 'Them going to fly out an' eeeeat you!' he sang, as soon as he heard she was going.

Mary sat. The train hadn't started going bang-a-lang yet, but it *was* making a *sshhhh-caaah* sound, like the devils were getting ready to wake up. She tried to calm herself by looking out of the window. People were moving busily back and forth, talking and lifting things: baskets and hampers and what her Auntie Greenie called scandal bags – because you could see through them – full of fruit and vegetables. A man rushed past, lugging a small goat under one arm. Mary giggled nervously.

'Tee-kets.' A man walked through the carriage, a little iron machine around his neck. His teeth were big white lumps in his mouth. He could hardly close it because it was so full.

Mary gave him her ticket like Auntie Greenie had said, and tried to smile when he smiled at her.

'You 'lone by you'self, girl?' said the ticket master.

'Yes, sir.'

Auntie Greenie told her she should call everybody 'sir', and that she should mind her peas and queues, which confused her a little. There had been queues at the train when Auntie Greenie came to see her away, but there had been no peas and she didn't like peas. Maybe the ticket master would try to give her peas? She watched his back meander down the train as her fist closed around the money pinned into her pocket. Thirty dollars in case of a 'mergency, and a piece of paper with her uncle's name and address in Aunty Greenie's fancy writing. Auntie Greenie had gone to a big school with lots of tall-haired people like herself. Mary didn't look like them, so maybe she looked like her daddy, but she'd never met him so she didn't know. Mary knew about the stoosh school because Auntie Greenie showed her old photographs. Rows of pretty light-brown girls standing with her aunt and Mary's mother, who was called Vi before she went away to America and left Mary with Auntie Greenie. Now she wrote letters and always signed her name Violet, not even Mamma. Auntie Greenie scolded Mary when she cried over the first letter.

'You mother have a nice white husband now,' she said. 'You must be happy for her.'

Auntie Greenie hadn't packed her any lunch and they'd forgotten breakfast because her aunt got up late, even though she had twice knocked politely on her bedroom door. Mary thought she would give her lunch money instead, but it seemed she'd forgotten that too. It was the helper's day off; *she* would have remembered. She was a nice fat lady.

She couldn't use the 'mergency money for food. She wasn't sure she knew what a 'mergency was. Her stomach hurt. Was that a 'mergency? Auntie Greenie was mean not to remember. After all, she *was* going away – *Forever More* – as Toby kept saying all month, in a big, scary voice. Toby was twelve, and he knew things. *Forever More* sounded like something for grownups, not what happened to a little girl. All morning she'd been trying to stop herself thinking about where she was going.

Montego Bay. To live with Uncle Barney. It didn't sound nice.

Toby had an opinion on this as well.

'*Country* Uncle Barney? You goin' turn into a ugly country gyal.'

'No I'm *not!*' she'd answered him back, but she didn't feel brave.

'Nobody don't like Uncle Barney. Him so ugly him have to run go country to find a wife.' Toby smacked his lips. 'Country fulla duppy too, and di whole ah dem stink like saltfish. When dem come at nighttime, dem suck out you spleen and you marrow, down to you bone-part.'

So, if she survived the train devils, there would be more to deal with. She would eventually get off the train, but who would save her at night? Uncle Barney would laugh if she got to country and talked about duppies, and his wife – who was probably an angry person because Uncle Barney was ugly – would be angry with *her*.

She had to remember what the helper said: that Toby told lies to get attention because nobody liked him. Which made her feel sad. And Auntie Greenie would never send her anywhere bad. Her aunt had a sharp tongue, but she let her make tamarind balls in the kitchen every Sunday, picking the tart, dark flesh off the fruit, sucking the sticky seeds until the top of her mouth burned. Then her aunt's friends came over and she was sent away with the top of a condensed milk can to soothe the mouth, because it was time to talk big people business.

She hoped Uncle Barney would have a nice house and that his angry wife wouldn't take her to church for *too* long.

The train hissed and she sat upright, fingers gripping the seat. She could see men and boys running up and down outside, banging the sides of the carriage. They were leaving. Mary squinched up her eyes and held her breath.

'Everybody come 'pon dis train now!' the ticket master yelled down the platform. Mary watched people scuttle into their seats with handfuls of chickens and green bananas and ackee and everybody talking at a great rate. Most of them were women.

'Lawd, my dear! Me never know waffi do when Berylou come to me yard lookin' fe her man…'

'Everybody come pon dis train *now*!'

'You want busta? Icy-mint? Suck-suck? Weh you want?'

'Anybody who nuh deh pon dis train *now* get lef ah Kingston!'

'Likkle girl, I goin' sit down right here. You mind?'

Mary stared. The man standing above her, smiling, reminded

her of an antelope from one of her schoolbooks. His legs were stretchy and thin and he wore a brown pinstripe suit. Best of all, he was wearing a tall red hat, an American daisy sticking out of the side. She couldn't speak. He was the most interesting-looking man she had ever seen. She could see that the women around them thought so too, as they were rolling their eyes and using their lips to point.

The interesting man stretched out his hand for her to shake. He had very long fingernails, like the bus conductors grew on their little fingers and then painted red. But these nails were silver, and they'd been shaped into wicked looking points, and there were little daisies painted on them.

'You don't mind?' asked the man. He was looking at her very seriously now, but it wasn't the glare of other grownups, hush you mouth and don't come inna big people business. He looked like he might just listen to what she said.

'Anybody can sit down here, sir,' she said. It was strange that an adult was asking her permission to do anything. It made her feel very grown up.

'Good!' The man sat down and continued to regard her, folding his legs underneath himself. He was smiling a smile of such beatific good will that Mary's chest felt fizzy, like when she drank too much ice cream soda.

'So you alright?'

'Yes, sir.'

'You is a *likkle* gyal.'

She wasn't sure what to say to that. People always said things that you could see in front of your face, and sometimes they said it twice. A fat man was *fat-fat*; a tall man was called Sky; the one-armed man was Oney; Auntie Greenie had a friend called Pot Cover, because of the shape of his forehead.

'Yes, sir.'

'So what you name?'

She was proud of her name.

'Mary Anne Bathsheba Clientele Switzie Pearl and Ezmereleena.'

The man smiled even wider.

'Brown,' she added.

The man seemed suitably impressed.

'Mary Anne Bathsheba Clientele Switzie Pearl *and* Ezmereleena Brown. Dat is one *rahtid* name.'

She liked him even more now. Auntie Greenie would have had him straight out of her house for the bad word, but Mary thought he was quite exciting.

'So what I must call you?' he asked.

Mary considered this. No one had ever asked her to choose. Only adults got to change Vi to Violet. She curled the baby hair at her temples, pretending to think. But she knew.

'Ezmereleena.' Mary was a boring church girl. But Ezmereleena would not be afraid of duppies or devils.

'Good!' The man clicked one silver finger against the other. 'And you can call me President Daisy.'

She stared at him. 'Um... dat is you name for true?'

He leaned forward. 'You see how you choose Ezmereleena? Well, me did choose President Daisy.'

She was confused. Everybody said never to question an adult, but this man wasn't like any adult she had ever met. 'What you is President over?'

President Daisy laughed. 'How you mean?'

'President have tings dem rule over. Like... like a country. Or a city.'

'But you smart! Well, I used to be President over Cockpit Country, but now I live in Montego Bay.' Something about that seemed to amuse him a great deal.

Mary realised that the train had already puffed out of the station, and it was going bang-a-lang, but she really couldn't believe that devils would dare hurt her while President Daisy was sitting nearby.

'You live inna Montego Bay?'

'Nearby there.'

He began to tell her about the countryside, but she found it difficult to concentrate on his stories as he swept his long arms around in circles. He had more dimples than she had ever seen on a person: two in one cheek, three in the other. Even his nose seemed to have a pleasant dip in its tip. His nails flashed in the sun as he spoke.

'When I was just your size, I used to go to river in de morning time, wash clothes wid mi madda. All I could see as I look over de place is green hills and people ah tell you *morning*. Dem forget how fe do dat inna de big city dem. Nuff-nuff pickney deh bout, play cricket, climb all big tree, ketch fish and croakin' lizard, and in de evening man and man play domino, roast fish an' breadfruit, eat till belly full. You ever stand under a waterfall, Ezmereleena?'

She shook her head.

'Auntie Greenie say I musn't put mi head under water.'

'Well, that is a shame. What else she said?'

Mary folded her hands and recited obediently.

'Remember to cream your skin a morning. Don't sit with your leg spread; that is not a lady. Don't eat and laugh, nor eat and drink at the same time. Chicken merry, hawk is near. You go to school to learn, not put on a fashion show. Don't talk too loud – we are not up in heaven straining to hear you. Badder dog than you bark, and flea kill 'im. Go to Sunday school and mind when preacher talk. Time is longer than rope. What sweet nanny goat, bound to run him belly –'

'Lord have mercy!' President Daisy interrupted. 'What a whole *load* of things for one girl-child, and what a good memory you have!'

Mary beamed and then exhaled in one big puff. She wished Toby could see her, travelling into *Forever More*, like a big girl. President Daisy was looking out of the window, humming to himself. She looked, too. They were running out of city, the last pieces of Kingston stretched out around them, tenement shacks topped with zinc sheets, like foil glinting in the sun. Up and down the carriage women continued loud discussions, mothers cuffed bawling children, mounds of produce threatened to burst and overflow into the corridors.

Mary's stomach, no longer distracted by fear, began to grumble again. A woman to her right sat with a tray of sweets between her knees. Mary craned her neck. Sticky Bustamantes, black with Demerara sugar; her beloved tamarind balls; coconut grater cakes all lumpy and pink on the top; gizzada tarts – her mother used to call them 'pinch-me-round'; Chinese sweeties in salt and sweet flavours – all scattered on a bed of humble blue icy-mints. Mary's mouth watered. Even one little icy mint would be so good. Her hand played with the money and instructions in her pocket. Auntie Green had written it down: 'If you uncle not there, take the 73 bus and ask them to put you off at The Church of Immaculate Conception. Go in and find the pastor. He will know you uncle. Barney might have run to country, but he is a God-fearing man.'

Surely Uncle Barney and his wife would remember to pick her up. She felt quite scared at the idea of a strange bus trip and a strange church.

'Missa Daisy, ahm, how much you think that lady selling tamarind ball for?'

President Daisy cocked his head to one side. 'Well, I don't rightly know. Mek we ask her. Lady!'

Her stomach lurched. She didn't want the woman to think she was definitely going to buy something. But it was too late. President Daisy was waving his long fingers. The woman swivelled her neck – and tray – to face them. She had been in deep discussion with the sullen man sitting next to her. He looked like he'd swallowed lime juice. The tray of sweets quivered.

'How much fi you tamarind ball?' asked President Daisy.

'Dollar fi three.'

'Dis little gyal want three.'

Dollar. No. She should keep the money safe. 'Missa Daisy –', but the woman was sorting through the tray.

'Me will give her six fi $1.50. Weh you seh?'

More money, now! The lady was haggling. This was worse. Mary put a hand on President Daisy's arm, but he was grinning and showing his dimples. '$1.70 fe six, throw two icy mint in deh.'

'Icy mint ah thirty cents fi one.'

'You lie! Since when? Two dollar buy five tamarind, two icy

mint, throw in a Busta.' President Daisy twinkled. The woman twinkled back. The sour man twitched.

The woman glanced at Mary. 'Look how she need fi fat-up! Is only one Busta she want? Five dollar get package deal: two tamarind, three icy mint, two Busta, one gizzada, plus a bag ah Chinese sweetie. Di salt one. Is lunch dat!'

'Lunch? Lunch mean chicken, man! Oxtail!'

They were up to five dollars! This was getting bad!

'Missa Daisy –'

'Me soon come, sweetheart. Mek me just fix dis ooman!' He twinkled some more. 'Pretty 'ooman like you, ah try tief a man?'

The woman reached inside her voluminous skirts. 'If ah lunch you ah look, me have chicken here. Ten dollar buy some good food. Look like *you* need it. What a man maaga!'

President Daisy roared with laughter. As the woman began to pile out what seemed like huge quantities of food onto the carriage floor, Mary glanced around for someone to help her stop the flow of barter. Maybe the sour man would help. He would have a good-looking face if he wasn't so miserable all the time. But the man looked even meaner now. His face was all puffed up, and his eyes moved back and forth between the woman and President Daisy.

The woman flourished several icy, multicoloured bags above her head. 'You want a suck-suck? It hot today, boy!'

President Daisy looked at her and laughed harder. 'You ah obeah 'ooman to rass! How you manage keep dem suck-suck cool? You have ice inna you baggie?'

'Eh-eh! Weh you know bout my crotches, boy?'

'All like *him* don't know nothing bout woman!' spat the sour man.

President Daisy fluttered his nails in a dismissive gesture. 'Now, Miss Lady, I'm lookin' two box lunch and three dollar sweetie fi me sweetheart, Ezmereleena.' He beamed at Mary. 'Don't worry, me have money.'

'Keep you money, bloodclaaht *batty* bwoy!'

The train froze. The lady clutched at her tray. 'Donovan,' she whined, 'you don't see me doin' business?'

'Shut up you mouth, gyal!' The woman ducked her head, all twinkle gone. Mary thought Donovan's face was even worse than before. It was two times bigger, and his eyes were shining dangerously. His whole body was swelling, chest forward, fists clenching. He wasn't as tall as President Daisy, but he was much bigger. And so *angry*.

Mary looked at President Daisy. His body had changed too. It was as if he'd gotten smaller, just for a moment, like he was wrapping himself deeper into his own skin. But when he spoke, Mary couldn't believe how calm his voice was.

'Boy. Quiet youself.'

It was too late. Donovan got to his feet. The sweetie tray teetered. Three tarts fell to the floor. Donovan crushed one under his heel. He was chanting now.

'Batty bwoy. Maama man. Suck hood bwoy. You love dem nastiness don't it, batty bwoy?'

'Ezmereleena,' said President Daisy. 'Put you fingers in you ears.'

She obeyed, disbelieving. The world became muffled. Why was the man being so mean to President Daisy? She could see both men's mouths moving. *I don't want to see any beating*, she thought. She took her fingers out of her ears. Not being able to hear them was worse than waiting on bang-a-lang devils in the train.

'Ah going *fuck* you up, bwoy!' Donovan snarled. He swung.

The women in the carriage shrieked.

President Daisy moved faster than anyone Mary had ever seen. He shifted to the right, unfolding himself out of his seat and past his attacker, all in one motion. His tall, red hat remained upright, serene and immovable.

Donovan's fist collided with the window, making a very satisfactory thwacking noise. He howled and cursed, cradling the wounded hand.

'Boy, I don't want to fight you.' President Daisy was at his full height now. People stared and clamoured. Donovan's woman croaked a protest. 'Leave de man in him personal business, Donovan!'

'Business? How you mean? Him fi *dead*!' Donovan lunged at President Daisy, who sidestepped him again, making him stumble. The carriage lurched. Donovan righted himself, grunted, and tried to hit him again. Mary realized that she was sucking her thumb. She took the offending digit away from her mouth. That was for *little* girls. She gulped, waiting for the meaty fist to connect with President Daisy's face. President Daisy stepped sideways. There wasn't much space, but he seemed able to move around it like a peeny-wally. Donovan roared in frustration. Mary felt like her head would break into little pieces.

Which is when President Daisy reached out and began to tickle the man.

It was the last thing anyone could have expected. First, the silver fingers in Donovan's solar plexus, as his hands went upwards in defence. His eyes bugged out of his head so hard, Mary wanted to laugh. Moving swiftly, his tongue stuck out in concentration, President Daisy danced his hands across his opponent's body, shoulders, stomach, running under his arms, down to his hips, across his neckbones, fingers flying as if he was playing a piano, always two steps ahead before the other man could push them away. Donovan was practically crying in frustration.

'You going to stop play with big man, boy?'

'*Batty* –'

'Alright, then. But if you play with big man, big man will play with you.'

'Ease off me, man! Don't touch me –'

'Or what?' President Daisy drew nearer. Donovan writhed and shrieked. President Daisy was holding one of his arms above his head, tickling his armpit. 'You *lucky* that woman and pickney deh bout.'

Tears streamed down Donovan's face. He began to beg. 'Please sir, please…' He had dropped to his knees, but still President Daisy stooped over him, forcing laughter and painful gasps out of him. Mary thought he looked angry for the first time and that was a bit scary.

'President Daisy!' she said, as loud as she could.

'You going back weh, boy? You going stop try frighten pickney?'

'Yeah, yeah!'

'Tell de likkle gyal you sorry. She name Ezmereleena.'

Chokes, gasps.

'Me sorry-me sorry-Ezmereleena. Me sorry!'

'Stop, President Daisy, *stop!*' said Mary.

President Daisy looked confused, as if he'd been somewhere else, not there. 'What?'

She stared at him. 'Stop tickle him now.'

It stopped. The American daisy on the hat swayed gently.

Donovan got to his feet, sweating profusely. He looked at President Daisy with something like awe. His sides heaved.

'You... you *touch* me.'

'Yes. A battyman touch you. Now go sit down in another carriage and take you woman with you and tell her nice things.'

Donovan scrambled backwards. The sweetie woman followed him more slowly. As she passed Mary, she dropped five sweets into her lap. She exchanged a look with President Daisy.

President Daisy nodded. 'Yeah.'

He sat down. His face seemed sad. Mary looked at him. All those things he said and Donovan said. It whirled around her head.

'Missa Daisy...'

'President.' His face looked like he might cry, and she wanted to hug him so he wasn't upset, but she didn't know how. 'I'm sorry, Ezmereleena.'

She reached out her hand. 'You want a tamarind ball?'

They sat, sucking the sweets, spitting seeds into their hands. Mary extricated a lump of sugar from her back tooth. President Daisy rubbed stickiness off his front teeth. The carriage went bang-a-lang. Soon she would be in Montego Bay, and there was nothing she could do about it. She put her hand on her jaw and sighed.

President Daisy looked at her. His face had gone all soft, like cotton. 'What happen?'

It came out in a flurry. 'My cousin Toby say dat country full up ah duppy and how dem smell bad and dem gwine come get me, an' I know de devil in di train not comin' while you is here, but de duppy going to definitely come for me and eat me spleen and I can't tell Uncle Barney or him wife because dem is church people and all dem going to say is *foooolishness*...' Her lip trembled. She was telling a stranger all this, but he had an American daisy in his red hat.

President Daisy patted her arm. 'Don't cry, Essy. Listen to me.'

She sniffed and tried to be brave.

'Yes,' he said. 'Country have duppy.'

That wasn't what she had expected at all. She put her thumb in her mouth.

'*But*,' President Daisy flung out an arm, 'when you see them at night time all you haffi do is stop an say howdy. People think seh them bad, but that is a lie.' He grinned at her. 'You know, whole heap of people think something bad, but is just because they don't have no experience with that thing. Me have *nuff* conversation with duppy and them never bother me yet. In *fact*, them smell like lady perfume.' He sat back with a satisfied smile on his face.

She couldn't believe it. A specialist in duppies!

'So... them not goin' to trouble me?'

'No, man. All you do if you see one is tell dem howdy, and dat you is President Daisy friend.'

★

She slept, then woke up when President Daisy shook her to say there were ten minutes left. She straightened her skirt and felt very alone indeed. She thought about how she didn't know Uncle Barney, and even less about his wife. She'd sent Auntie Greenie an Easter bun last Christmas, with sultanas and wrapped in a yellow bow. A woman like that might be nice to her. But she'd also heard that women didn't like strange girls in their houses. Auntie Greenie's friends said so. Trouble was sure to follow when too many hen live in a rooster pen. Her mother had worked as a helper for her American husband before he divorced his wife, so she was already known as trouble. With a mother like that.

The train hissed, slowing.

Maybe Uncle Barney's wife would think she was trouble too.

'No devil came out of the train then,' said President Daisy.

'No,' she said. But she could feel the tamarinds in her tummy, making her sick.

'Montego Bay, final stop, final stop!' sang out the ticket master.

Silver nails folded themselves over her small hands.

★

Uncle Barney was smaller than she thought he would be, although he did have coolie hair and big eyes. He also had a sign with her name in big letters: WELCOME! MARY! BROWN! He was smiling wide.

'Welcome,' said Uncle Barney. He pulled her into his arms and hugged her. He smelt comforting. Like lady's perfume. He was telling her how brave she was to come on the train by herself, such a pretty, brave little girl. She looked around. No sign of a scary wife. She looked up at President Daisy, who was standing above them both. The cotton wool look was back, so soft and nice.

'This is my friend, President Daisy,' she said to her uncle. 'He tickled a bad man on the train.'

'Did he now?'

Most of the people who got off the train were gone and the platform was nearly empty. The air smelled like mango. She watched a bright green parrot rustle in a tree nearby, then fly to another, squawking excitedly. She looked back at the men. They were standing, watching her, smiling.

They were holding hands.

'Her name isn't Mary. It's Ezmereleena,' said President Daisy.

She looked at the sign with her old name. It was red, and heart-shaped, and covered with little American daisies.

## MINTY MINTY

Jeannie Smith bought the baby from the smiling woman for everything in her purse: twenty-three pounds, one hundred and seven US dollars, and a photo of her mother, posing under a blurry Christmas tree. She liked the picture because her mother looked peaceful, which was rare.

The smiling woman handing over the baby said she was pleased to see that Jeannie's mother was an African woman. 'You look like toubab,' she said, grinning so wide her teeth fought, using the local name for a white person, gesturing at Jeannie's pale skin.

Jeannie was used to the confusion. She'd come out of her mother's belly pale – prize to her father's Irish heritage. So she was Arabic in the Middle East, Hispanic on New York streets, black to white people. She'd hoped that on her first visit to an African nation, they'd recognize her pedigree. Notice that her hair was a bit too bad, too fluffy. That they'd see her Mamma-Africa roots in the twist of her hip, but no. Since she'd arrived a week ago, she'd been toubab along with all the other British tourists, despite their blondness and freckles, and she'd burned under the stern sun with the rest of them.

The baby in her arms was unmistakably black. Jeannie had never seen a baby with pronounced cheekbones, but this one had them, along with a beach-ball belly and thin arms. She looked like a live version of those charity ads you saw on TV. She was the tiniest little person, just perfect. The smiling woman gestured: 'She good, strong baby. Make you happy in London, toubab.'

★

The woman had spotted them arriving in the village after a three-hour journey. Jeannie's ass was stuck to the hot seat, her hair stood up at mad angles, her stomach and arms hurt from clinging to the hurtling van and she was the dirtiest she'd ever been in her life. A thick red layer of dust had made them all the same colour. The only creatures unencumbered by the dust were the black flies whizzing around her face, arms and ankles. But she was OK. Hadn't Leonardo diCaprio said it in that movie, *Blood Diamond*? TIA, darling. This Is Africa. This was a poor country; people didn't do things the way she was used to. She was sure they would be appalled at Londoners: falling out of clubs, shrieking and vomiting; lack of sunshine; tube dirt in your nostrils and off the newspaper print. TIL, darling. This Is London.

★

The baby girl blinked and squirmed. Jeannie traced a finger over her face, smelled the curved head, a protective surge in her chest visceral and surprising. She dipped forward, kissed the damp brow. Who says she can't? Who says? She was aware this was mad. There would be questions, officials, investigation, surely?

The smiling woman mimed the most intimate of motions: she wanted something else. Jeannie stared. The woman repeated the movement. *My knickers*, thought Jeannie. Dreamily, she turned away, hiked up the material, hooked her thumbs into the French knickers from Marks and Spencer's. She'd given up g-strings three years ago, after another transient lover said that her stomach was peeking out around the edges. French knickers, they would do. They were grownup underwear.

Her head spun as she handed over the creamy lace, embarrassed at its dampness and flavour.

The smiling woman took the bounty, examined. Sniffed. Jeannie turned away. The hut was a single room, dirt floor, taken up with the tat she's seen all over the country: oddly porcine tigers; tie-dyed cloth that reminded her of her Jamaican grandmother; cheap beads and bracelets she could get for a pound in south London.

She wanted none of it.

She wanted this little girl.

★

She told everyone she was going to Africa for her birthday. Alone, they asked. Alone! But it would be such a spiritual journey! They fluttered over the brochures. It was important to have luxury. She was turning forty, after all. Five-star, but there would be excursions. This was the one she'd looked forward to most: a cruise down the golden river, the booklet said. Then through the village to meet the elders, the museum, and onto the island, one of the outposts where they'd sent her ancestors as slaves into the Middle Passage. She'd wanted to cry, just thinking about it. She imagined standing on the island, cool breeze at her head, then plunging, horrified, into echoing dungeons.

It hadn't been like that. The package deal was a rip-off. Instead of a cruise they were loaded onto a ferry so bursting with vehicles that every rock and murmur threatened a watery grave, where people squatted and pissed in front of each other. Then onto a rickety, open-air jeep. They bounced past a stinking abattoir, complete with a vulture council, pecking strips off suppurating carcasses of goats and sheep. She couldn't smell anything, realised she'd been mouth-breathing for hours. The knowledge embarrassed her, as if she'd looked at her African brothers and sisters and automatically held her nose.

And the island. She was appalled to feel nothing much at all. One of the tourists kept up a stream of questions throughout the

inarticulate tour: 'This was where they brought them?' 'Whipped
them?' 'Held the rebels?' 'Do you Africans still feel angry? When
you think of what we did to you?'

'No boss, no boss,' said the tour guide, bobbing and weaving.
'Now we live in harmony together, black and white. Like Michael
Jackson.'

Frustrated, Jeannie had turned her face up to the sky, hoping
for a rush of spiritual fervour. But she was too hot and her head
was pounding and she could feel her forehead burning in the sun.

She hadn't put on sun tan lotion. Too black for that.

*I'm an idiot*, she thought.

Later, when she asked for a toilet, the second guide, a boy of
no more than seventeen, pushed a curl off her sweaty cheek back
behind her ear, said it was silky, and invited himself back to her
hotel. Bring back a man, her girlfriends said. Or have some fun.

'I could be your mother,' she scolded him.

He smiled, shrugged.

★

The smiling woman took out a surprisingly fat breast and offered
it to the baby, who fastened on. *It's her last meal*, Jeannie thought.
The feeding woman fanned away a fly.

★

The hotel was beautiful. Entering reception, she could see the
ocean through the huge window in front of her; it was as if she
could walk straight from her life into the belly of the Atlantic. She
snapped hundreds of photos of the flowers just outside her door.
Each day began with a beach walk, marvelling at the rich rubbish
coughed up by the sea: squid, huge fish, beige and cream shells,
jellyfish; once, a grand, hulking dead turtle. Plastic bags, a flip-
flop encrusted with tiny sea creatures. The gulls were fat and men
took white cows for walks. The sea was angrier than she'd
expected – no azure Greek perfection, this; it was grey-blue, like

a Southampton sky, and full of seaweed shadows. Beyond that, clean, clear water. If only she could swim past the crap.

★

'I'm not supposed to think like this,' she murmured. The smiling woman blinked at her, jerked the baby awake from its milk-drugged stupor. She gasped, whimpered, began to suckle again. *Fill your belly*, Jeannie thought. She'd given the woman all the cash she had. A credit card would have to do the rest. She did sums in her head. Money to the driver of the jeep, money to the concierge. Money got everything here, right?

'You know I'm forty today?' she said to the mother, who gazed at her. 'Forty,' she says, pointing to herself. 'Today.'

'Yes, yes,' said the woman. She looked bored. Jeannie felt a prickle of annoyance. Perhaps she didn't understand.

All year she'd been saying to colleagues and strangers, casually, nearly forty this year, the big one, it's coming. No, they all said. Even one of the tourists, today: 'God, you look good on it.' A teenage couple in the jeep had blinked, confused. Too young.

The baby's nose was running, which didn't detract from its cuteness. Surely that was love. The mother shifted the little girl to her second breast and waved at her bric-a-brac. 'You buy, lady? All for you. Mix blood toubab price.' Necklaces. A broken shell and a sculpture of Bob Marley. Why was she looking? Her money was gone. The guide outside was calling her name. They were coming back from the "Journey of No Return" exhibition. She'd balked at the front steps, at the large sculpture of a slave couple, chained together, at awkward angles. It looked as if the man was beating the woman. That was when the smiling woman came up to her. 'You buy baby, lady? Special price.'

★

She felt sweat between her bare thighs as she took the child, swiftly, cradled her, moving towards the jeep. She'd sit in the front. This Is Africa, and this baby was strong. She'd manage the bumping journey. She, Jeannie would protect her.

★

When the guide explained there was no luxury river cruise – the guidebook old, old – he'd offered them bulging packs of cheap sweets, instead. Lollipops, bubblegum, indeterminate suckable things: brightly coloured sugar. 'There will be hundreds of children calling out to you,' he explained. 'Give them this.'

The other tourists took them easily; Jeannie didn't know why she refused. It was only later she understood. In the first village, the children ran screaming towards them, hands outstretched, resplendent rags, little knees pumping frantically. 'Helloooo, helloooo,' they cried, like the sound of high-pitched birds, palms up and pleading. 'Minty, minty,' they called. The tourists threw the sweets out, into hands, bouncing off heads, and the children scrabbled in the dirt. Jeannie recoiled. It was like feeding animals at the zoo. She wanted to scream, stop! Tears in her eyes. She turned to the woman beside her – 'Do you?' – but the woman was throwing out yellow and blue and red lollipops. Only the teenage couple seemed to understand her distress. The boy kissed his teeth, dropped his sweets into his lap and crossed his arms.

There were nine villages and through each one, the same macabre ritual. Helloooo-helloooo, minty minty, and the laughing British and Americans and the shame at her temples.

'Don't know why you're moaning,' said one woman, even though Jeannie hadn't said anything. 'All kiddies like sweets. Like Halloween, innit?'

★

Jeannie strode towards the jeep. Her bare thighs felt strong. One arm cradled her baby, the other waved in the air, keeping the flies at bay. They were all staring at her, but she ignored them.

She knew she looked good for forty, she didn't need their approval.

'Give me the front seat,' she murmured to the younger guide, the one who wanted to sell himself to her. His face cracked open, his eyes and mouth round, but he opened the door. She settled, shifted the baby, felt warm wetness against her chest. No nappies. There'd be time for that. 'Back to the ferry!' she called, through the sliding glass window. 'Everyone ready?' She was aware that they were staring very hard, but that wasn't her concern. The baby was smiling and she smelled very good, smelled like earth and ancestors.

A woman she didn't recognise broke through the small and gathering crowd. She was speaking rapidly in Wolof, gesticulating and screaming, pointing at Jeannie. 'Toubab!' she said over and over. 'Toubab takes my baby!'

★

Jeannie cried all the way back to the hotel, through the reception, down the steps to the beach, under the cooling sky. She sat among the squid and the gorging gulls and eventually slipped into the ocean water and swam past the seaweed.

'Minty minty,' she whispered. 'Helloooo, helloooo.'

### BREATHING

On Tuesday the world went mad.

Or perhaps it was me. Whatever the case, that was the day my dead wife came back. It was a normal morning, if normal is the word for the seventy-sixth day after your wife gets hit by a large, moving vehicle and is suddenly dead.

DEAD.

I played with the word in my head until it bounced there permanently, in letters made of yellow rose petals, like the flowers on her grave. I was doing that the morning Val came back. It was about 3 am. She knew I'd be awake. I was already an insomniac. It didn't get worse after she died – not like in books where the protagonist drips his agony into beer bottles and develops bags under his eyes. I looked pretty much the same. It was just that the nights seemed longer and I hadn't cried yet and the word kept bouncing.

★

I was sitting in bed, reading *The National Enquirer* – my choice of reading material verged between Kafka, old Alice Walkers and shit magazines these days – when the doorbell rang. *Bing. Bong.* I thought about how Val had hated that sound and how I'd come home one day and she'd been trying to change it to some kind of wimpy wind-chime, but all she'd managed to do was rip out bits of the door, and I thought, hey-ho, I should be fixing that door, and any day now I will, just as soon as someone tells me my wife isn't D-E-A-D. Then I went and opened the door.

At first I couldn't see her because the yellow letters were in the way, but eventually my eyes cleared. There she was. Val. Looking very calm, with her hair in two kid's plaits like she wore in bed at night. Val never did like weaves.

'Hi,' she said.

'Hi,' I said. Someone had picked me up and put me in the freezer. I clung to the door jam.

'You haven't fixed the door, bwoy,' she said. Val always called me 'bwoy' in her pretty Jamaican accent.

'Yes,' I said. I closed my eyes and watched the yellow letters pop and dissolve. I opened them and she was still there. Two plaits, the black dress I buried her in, and that slow smile.

'I'm kinda thirsty…' she murmured.

I took her to bed. I had to, you see. It was a private joke, between us – what Val said when she wanted sex. 'I'm kinda *thirsty*,' she'd say, and there was the smell of woman in that tiny sentence. So I took her to bed, fresh from the grave. I heard a lot of men did that when the world went mad and the dead came back to us. I wonder what that means.

After I took my wife – every tiny piece and pore of her – spread her over my body and mewed inside her ear, I let her hold me as I cried. I couldn't stop. She was breathing, steadily. It was the sweetest sound.

'It's weird for me too,' she said.

'Yes,' I said. The tears were at the back of my eyes, roaring like a river. I couldn't look at her.

She grabbed my face. 'Cut out the damn *shock*, Jeff. I think I'm OK, but if *you* freak out, *I'm* gonna freak out –' Her lips trembled. 'Please. I *need* you.'

The roaring sound stopped. How long did I have – to talk to her, to touch her? Maybe this was a one-shot deal, a twenty-four hour Return of the Zombie Lover. I had to be present as long as it lasted. And she needed me. Of course she did. After all, it was she who was dead.

'Val, *what the fuck*?'

'I don't know!' she said.

'I *saw* you dead!'

'I know, right?' she said. 'The last time I saw you was March 22nd. You wouldn't go out for the *bloodclaaht* milk and I thought about why I ever married you.' She laughed, shakily.

I laced my fingers between her plaits and her scalp: so warm, so alive. 'You're not hurt, I mean, there aren't any...'

'...wounds.' She finished it for me. 'Was it bad?'

Yeah, Val. It was bad. They covered you and treated you, but I looked. At the raw edges of your stomach. Your insides, out. It was as if the truck rolled over you, tore you in half, then came back for more. But I didn't say that.

'Not too bad, baby,' I said.

She knew I was lying. Passed my hand over her tummy. Like a chalkboard going soft, unmarked, but not new. Like before she left. I grabbed an inch, fiercely. *Pinch her, you'll wake up*, I thought. It didn't work. She giggled, then she was serious. 'The last thing I remember... you trying to grab me. I didn't see the truck and you tried so *hard* –'

I put my hand up to her mouth, letting her breath stir the tips of my fingers.

'Where did you go, Val?'

'Hell,' she said, simply.

Outside, we could hear the sound of sirens, wailing into the morning. There were a lot of them.

★

We watched the morning news. It was frightening. Shots of people running around the streets. Burning vans. ('Why would you burn vans?' asked Val). Interviews with several teenagers. ('Yeah man, we think it's coo-wul our dad's back!') But you could see the nervous tics on everybody. It was happening all over the world. At approximately 3 am, everybody's dead had come back, as simple as that. There only seemed to be one corpse per family, but who knew what was going to happen next? The God-botherers beseeched Him for help in the pulpits, beamed out by FOX. Shrinks had a field day. Pretty soon CNN was interviewing corpses at the rate of one every 9.3 seconds. We timed it.

They all looked pretty normal. Like Val. No wounds. Perhaps a slight faraway look in the eyes. But nothing you could put a finger on, while continents declared states of emergency. One congressman asked if 'they' would be allowed to vote. Another talked worriedly about food stocks and freaking immigration. He had spittle on his lips and sweat on his chin. Later we heard it was his mother that came back and he hadn't liked her much.

'That won't be a problem,' said Val, watching him.

'What?'

'I don't think we get hungry.'

★

She told me about Hell. It was bad. As confusing and hard to grasp as a dream – and changing all the time. She was forced to hunt food for a family. They were like something out of a bad dinosaur movie, all jaws and eyes and smell. They beat her. They told her to grab the rabbits that ran along nearby rock-faces, grab them by the ears and bash them over the head. She'd put two rabbits in a plastic zip-lock bag, their snuffling noses pressed hard against the clear plastic, hearts beating fast. She closed her eyes and swung them as hard as she could against a wall, but nothing happened, and horrified, she let them go.

I passed my hands up and down her smooth arms, aching, but there was more. She was in Central Park running from rape gangs. It felt as if the world had imploded. She had no understanding that she was dead, just that she was surrounded by insane revellers, handfuls of pink and blue pom-poms, all wanting to hurt her. Hiding under bushes, bruised and terrified, she wondered where I was. Had I survived? How could she find me?

By the time she did, she was nothing more than a disembodied head and fingernails, dragging herself along the ground like a slug, outside our apartment, clawing the walls, coughing up dust as I stood above her, opening my chest with a knife, trying to stem the flow of my blood.

Whoever created Hell knew her better than she knew herself. Animals, rape, me.

Hell: a personalised service.

She wanted to watch *The Sopranos* on HBO, but there was nothing on except news.

★

I took the most unashamed sick leave of my life. I didn't care that I'd just got back to the classroom. I loved the kids, but screw them. I mean, how often do you get a second chance at the love of your life, right? And the same love, the one you knew was working for you, even in between petty bickering and slight disagreements about how to bring up children and when to have them and what to say to them about religion, sex and food additives. So I called Burt, my boss. A good man; he'd always done his best by his staff.

'I'm taking two weeks,' I said.

He cleared his throat. 'Val, right?'

I said yes. Then, because I had to: 'Who'd you get?'

He paused. 'No-one. I thought it would be one of my parents. They're the only ones…' He cleared his throat again. None of us had worked out a language yet, a way to speak about the dead that didn't sound like the kind of lies and platitudes spoken by the graveside.

'Yeah,' I said.

He paused. 'Jeff…'

I waited. His voice sounded like he'd been gargling with nails. 'Is she… is she… you know… *alright*?'

He meant something different, I think. He wanted to ask me whether she was rotting across our kitchen floor, whether she smelled bad, if she slithered under the bed at night or howled at the moon.

'She's fine,' I said. Because it was true.

'Yeah,' he said. 'So, a fortnight, and we'll see how you feel?'

'Thanks.' I felt the need to comfort him. 'If… if anyone comes I'm sure they'll be OK too, Burt.'

He laughed, but it was strained. 'I hope so.'

★

We played like kids. We got romantic. We'd always done the candlelight dinners and the walks in the rain and the making love as much as busy lives let us, but now nothing delighted me more than normal stuff. Watching my wife cut her toenails, pretending she wasn't chewing the clippings. Watching her hack apart pieces of oxtail for that stew I hated, but she didn't care and made it every month. Watching her gossip on the phone with her girlfriends – one of them was back from the grave as well and this delighted her beyond measure. They talked a lot about being dead. Her girlfriend had gone through three abortions before she was twenty, and in her Hell her children had floated around her, screaming accusations and begging for their lives. Val cried when she heard that. 'My God, that is *exactly* the thing that would upset her the most,' she said. 'What did we ever do to deserve that as an afterlife? I mean, forever?'

We talked. We'd always done that, never stopped, all the way through meeting, courtship, engagement, through fights and squabbles and loving. It had been essential for this love affair between a Brooklyn boy and a girl from Jamaica. We talked to create frames of reference, to translate culture, to explain away stereotypes. To love each other. It was the kind of relationship I'd only dreamed of before I met her.

I knew she wasn't rotting because she told me – Wednesday, about 2 pm: 'Jeff – look like I don't need lotion no more. Maybe dead good for dry skin!' Tuesday, one week gone: 'So what, I never going to get a period again? I was due. You think it all dry up inna the grave?' And my favourite, one night, staring into the bedroom mirror: 'Jeff, come and look! My eyes keep changing colour!' They did, too, from then on. Greens and blues and a curious kind of aubergine, and yellow one morning when she woke up and demanded toast and eggs – not because she was hungry, for she had no appetite – but because, 'Lawd, I might as well eat at the table with you, baby. After all, I never did learn to wait for hungry *then*, so why give up the food now, especially when it taste so sweet?'

I was wrong to say that the dead weren't different. They were. It was as if death had made everything better. My wife's skin gleamed. There was nothing more beautiful than Val, sticky with spare ribs and gravy, sitting in our back yard, calling to the neighbours, laughing uproariously with Mr Charles, a sixty-something liberal who'd come back from the dead quick enough to practically cry at the too-close-to-call jokes and George Dubya Bush in power. 'I can feel everything so much more,' she tried to explain. And it seemed to be true for all of them. You could pick out a dead person on the street from a hundred yards because they looked so goddamned happy. Dead-stare, we all started calling it. They tripped along like they were walking on air. Like they were all real happy just to be there. And I suppose that made sense.

★

I dreamed the accident; I daydreamed the accident. The awful, wrenching shriek of the brakes and the last *blam!* a kind of wet sound, and I remembered thinking: *Those are her muscles, her flesh, that's her bones breaking, that's it, the end. The end.* I didn't want to think about it, but I thought about it.

★

Three weeks in, one morning, I reached over to her as I usually did. She rolled closer; she was in the mood, I could tell from the way she sighed through the tiny gap between her front teeth and got all silky under my hand. Traced my spine. Fingers searching, feeling, moving. I moved between her legs, smelling her. Fingers at my shoulder blades, thrumming.

'Jeff…'

'Hmm?'

She shifted, raised herself on her elbows. I blinked.

'What?'

She pushed at me, making me lie on my stomach. I grinned, hard-on twitching. Still the fingers down my spine.

'Look at how the muscles curve through your body,' she cooed.

There was something odd about the tone of her voice. I'd really never heard her talk quite like that.

'It's perfect. I wish you could see it. How the muscles curve. They fit, like a jigsaw.'

'Um…' My erection was wilting. 'Baby, I'm glad you think I'm so beautiful, but…'

'Oh, not just *you*,' she said. 'All people. All the bodies, just perfect.'

Bemused, I lay down again. 'A massage would be nice…' I murmured into the pillow.

'Just a minute, man. I just want to look.'

I laughed, nervously. 'And not touch?' Though I wasn't sure I wanted her to touch me anymore. Not with my face in the pillow.

'Oh, I'm touching.' Her fingers almost burned. 'Just give me a minute.'

I relaxed a little; her touch was familiar again. It was silly to be nervous. Of what? Of Val, who'd ripped through Hell looking for me? But there was a ball of something frozen in my chest, even as I dozed off under her ministrations. When I woke up, she was gone.

I climbed out of bed and found her in the backyard, chewing a pear. She was gleaming and dishevelled, chewing with her eyes closed, head thrown back, as if she was listening for something.

'Val?'

Silence. Ecstatic chewing. The ball in me hadn't melted. It was growing, threatening to fill my belly.

'Val?'

'What?'

'What are you doing?' She looked so sweet. But so distant.

'Eating a pear.'

'I can see that. Want to come in for breakfast?'

'The pear's sweet.'

'Yes.' I didn't know what else to say.

She chewed on. I watched her for a while, then went to eat breakfast alone.

★

My head filled with images, sounds and blood. Memories of that morning. I'd known she was pissed that I wouldn't go for the milk, and so I'd followed her as she banged the apartment door shut. I hit the front steps as she strode away from me, head down, muttering: 'Bloodclaaht *man* cyaan go get *milk*, imagine, *milk* weh *him* drink every morning...'

So she didn't see the truck as she stepped into the road.

It was sudden, like a trick. Clear your throat and it was there, like a graceful animal. And in the moment she stepped off the sidewalk I knew she wasn't going to stop, and I knew that the truck driver wouldn't see her in time. I could feel my muscles rushing. I ran track in high school, and it was that rush that comes two seconds before the whistle, the moment when you ask your body to fly and it coils into obedience.

I flew.

Time is a strange thing. I could see the seconds racing and rushing by, an urgent countdown. I could not fail. I could *see* myself, pushing my wife across the street, see her stumbling, falling, scraping her knees and hands, eyes wide, safe.

And then I saw me, a rag doll, in the body of the truck, dwarfed and soft. Could feel the smash and the promise of oblivion. That's when I chose to abandon her. It wasn't like she remembered it.

If you had asked me, over dinner, replete with wine, whether I'd give my life to save my wife, I would have said yes in a fraction of a second. Bring on the asshole with the gun, the mortal combat, the poisoned chalice: me, first! But a fraction of a moment is a pure thing, and new temptations arise. And I didn't want to die.

So I chose. I timed my grab, like pulling a punch back to soften the connection. I knew my hand would flail in the breeze, close, but not close enough to save Val. Just the right distance to save me from that truck. *Miss her*, my mind screamed. *Don't die*.

And then the sound of body hitting metal and wire and the sound of her wailing my name.

★

My wife doesn't talk to me anymore. She is lost in minutiae. She spends her time listening to sounds in the breeze, covering her hands in engine oil, eating a pear all day, reading a single sentence over and over again, sighing in pleasure. Her body sparkles. She has no wounds. She pays no attention to me, and it breaks my heart.

I listen to the silence around me. It's a perfect silence. I remember the sweet sound of Val breathing when she came back to me. I remember her wailing my name. I listen for my own breath, but I realise that nothing is there. Now that I turn to my own body, I notice, suddenly, that there is no rise or fall of my chest. Only a curious crunching of bone. I rattle. I think my legs are broken. My neck clicks and echoes. Perhaps it is broken too. I found a piece of wire in my thigh last night. And I am so cold.

No matter.

In her Hell, she was raped, she tried to kill bunny rabbits, her body was reduced to a monstrosity, her husband killed himself in a shower of gore. All very female concerns, you understand. Not surprising, really. A personalised service, you remember.

I don't care about being dead.

It's just that Val won't talk to me anymore. She won't talk to me anymore.

She won't talk to me.

## PHONE CALL TO A
## LONDON RAPE CRISIS CENTRE

We are physically, sexually, intellectually entwined. He taught me that people matter in some ways but not in others. That feeling is not a cliché. He taught me how to tear apart poetry and then fix it; how to watch people; how to give up and start again. He taught me fellatio, and pretended in his turn that my body was edible; hummed northern soul when he sucked my toes, screamed when he climaxed and cried in his sleep. Coffee is just coffee, but when he made it, it warmed my lips and the smell...

We had children, but only pretend. It did matter that people whispered. Sometimes we hid away from the gossip. Sometimes we kissed in public, hips grinding, wetness spreading, then ran, laughing, before we were caught. I wore pink ribbons longer than was ever seemly.

He made sure I did my homework, bandaged my scrapes and gave me all the pets I ever owned. I bounced on his lap. At night he rolled me into a ball and tucked himself into the edges.

His wife never understood him. She never understood me, either. I'm the only good thing that ever came out their marriage.

We do have fun.

We do.

## VELVET MAN

Ghosts know who best to haunt. An old Jamaican friend once told her that. She thinks about this idea a lot, after the velvet man leaves. About what it is to be drawn to something just for you: a perfectly fashioned event, a person, or a moment. It is the kind of thing that people write about – this flawless sense of fate – but she'd never understood it. She was a sensible woman. Better to do your nails, steam your face and cook for the week on a Sunday. To read the material two weeks in advance of the meeting, then a few days before to refresh the memory: that was success. To buy pak choi in the local market and better quality cuts of meat at the butcher; extra money-saving lightbulbs; keep numbers for the plumber and the local hot-line for nuisance neighbours by the phone; insure the dog.

Iron your skirt, because.

★

She was late for work that morning, smoothing her fingers over her knees and her well-ironed blue skirt when the velvet man entered the empty train carriage, sat down right next to her – when he might have taken any of twenty other battered, orange and blue patterned seats available – and murmured something softly under his breath.

She was not troubled in the first few seconds, nor even

surprised at his long limbs or his sudden proximity. If forced to say, she might have explained that it felt like an old friend had wandered onto the train, after years of absence, and she'd recognised his saunter or the back of his head.

The man murmured again. His eyes made her think of those black velvet paintings that were all the craze in the seventies. Her mother had kept two in the drawing room, one of John Wayne, the other of five dachshunds playing poker. When she was a child she'd been smacked more than once for pulling a chair up below them so she could stroke their soft edges.

'Pardon me?' she said to the velvet man.

He smiled. She could smell his healthy, wheaty breath, took in his thick, white-blonde hair and his large hands that were spread over his denim knees. She looked down at his clean, well-shaped fingernails. Those eyes: oddly black where you'd really expect blue, given his colouring. She might poke her finger inside and suck something sweet off the tip of it.

'Tell me what I can do for you,' he said.

His face was open; eyes steady and perfectly calm. It was a kind face, and she thought there was a sort of bravery in exposing that to a stranger. She opened her mouth to ask him all the obvious questions – who are you, don't talk to me, move away, what could you possibly mean? She could feel where the muscles in her wrists and thighs should be tensing for movement up out of her seat and away.

Instead, she paused. He was joking, of course. It was mere hyperbole – like those Nigerian men who told you they were princes in their countries; or like a new song that runs out of steam after it started so well.

'Tell me what I can do for you,' the velvet man said patiently.

His expression was solemn, watching her carefully, as if this might be the most important thing he would say today, or this week.

Suddenly, hotly, she considered the idea. The deliciousness, the expansiveness of it assailed her. She could be important, different; she felt a lurching in her chest. She was late on the train, heading for ordinary: the job, the lunch-break, the colleagues, the wishes, the dreams, all so irreparably dull and chipped.

The train pushed into the station and she knew what she wanted – at least, where to begin. She grabbed his hand; he rose up with her, and there was joy on his face.

★

The market was in full swing with mid-morning bargains, the scrape of bottles and boxes, smells of best meat and fish, and she'd never seen the city sky so blue, amplifying every blush in the arcade: melons hacked open, sides of salmon strewn with black peppercorns; strawberry tarts glistening in syrup.

And the peonies at the flower stall.

She came to an abrupt stop in front of them, dropping the velvet man's hand, tucking her palms together like a little girl, teeth in her bottom lip. She was rocking slightly, almost breathless. Her parents had thought cut flowers a bourgeoisie affectation.

She looked up at the velvet man: he was beaming, waiting.

'But of course,' he said.

More flowers, she thought later, than anyone had ever got in the world. Armfuls of the pink peonies first, because she liked their little cabbage faces peeping up at her; fat roses next, ringed in sprays of eucalyptus, and the velvet man instructed the flower stall owner to make sure every thorn was taken off. He'd opened his mouth to say you're having a laugh, mate, but then the velvet man gave him enough money to make him grin and set his assistant picking. Urged on by both men now, she chose huge daisies the size of her hand, laughing delightedly; a long box of cerise anthuriums, their bright plasticky stamens reminding her of hot places.

'Happy?' asked the velvet man, when all were chosen and she stood, sticky with sap and ever so slightly breathless at her own excess. She hesitated. He was still smiling, gently leaning down to move a leaf from her hair.

'Yes,' she said. 'Thank you. So generous. Thank you so much.'
'And now…?'
His bow was near-genuflection. She stared.
'What?'
'Whatever you want.'

★

She was the kind of woman who had always paid her way. Paid her half of the meal, despite her date's protests. Not that there had been a million men in her life. She had an ordinary face and an easily concealed body, so there had been no more than a few gently drunken fumbles before Jack, at uni. She knew she could have gathered many more sexual experiences: a plain girl was easy, by necessity. But she was determined not to be seen in that way; invisibility was the better choice.

Jack was bearded and fairly ordinary himself: unexpectedly judicious in his courting. The first time they had sex he lost and gained his erection three times, sawing back and forth inside her so long that his eventual orgasm had them both mistaking relief for love.

★

She wanted to see things, do things, new things. The velvet man slid them into an black car sleek with butter-soft upholstery.

A private viewing of several complex and beautiful paintings, he guiding her from one piece to another, pointing out colour, texture, inviting her thoughts. She knew nothing of modern art, but as he smiled and shared his own pleasure in the work, she slowly began to say what she saw, felt, loved.

The velvet man hired a helicopter so they could zoom low over the city, snug together in the belly of a huge bumblebee, yelling happily over the roar of the blades. Below her, the city looked bleak and cheerless, and she was momentarily frightened, making herself small under the velvet man's armpit. He smoothed the soft hair at her temples and squeezed her hand, yelling almost angrily at the pilot: 'Take us down!'

'No,' she said, 'can we just see something pretty?'

'Close your eyes,' he said, 'I'll tell you when,' and she might have dozed against his chest, or through some deeper reverie, and then the city was behind them and they were to-ing and fro-ing above green hills, watching silver-blue rivers pour deep into tiny valleys. She wondered if they disturbed the birds, and at the softness of the velvet man's skin over his chest and arms.

'Happy?' he asked.

'Yes,' she managed to say, her cold cheek against his good shirt.

'I'll do anything you want,' he said.

★

Jack had broken off with her in the second year, to sleep with a more intelligent woman, she suspected, then come back with his tail between his legs the term afterwards. She'd punished him for just long enough and then they'd stayed up late studying for finals in her neat and polished room – he politics and history, she marketing. They had married two years later; divorced seven years after that. There had been no children, a fact that relieved her nearly as much as the sight of his slightly sweaty-shirted back walking out of their small, well-organised apartment, hands gripping two suitcases she'd refused to pack for him, then packed anyway, and a large teddy bear he'd had since childhood. The divorce was uncomplicated, as such things go.

All the way through their courtship and lives together, she'd had jobs, maintained her own chequing account and independence; paid half the bills. She had decided to be the best of modernity: she would not be hoe or a bitch or a gold-digger or a floozy – or what did they call them these days? Thots and skanks and ratchet girlies. No. That kind of woman offended her. The rampant consumerism even more than the exchange of flesh.

★

A spa was next: entry via a discreet doorway off an expensive street. He waited patiently in the quiet foyer as she was taken away and stripped: washed first in sprays of perfumed water, a salt scrub applied, then thick, warm cinnamon oil ladled all over her body and rubbed in; more water to finish; the gentle breathing of the two women working on her tight neck, her loose calves. She had always been thin and relatively fit, but under their ministrations she felt like a crust of something – stale bread, a discarded piece of a pie. A sliver of something they were trying to render pliable.

One of the girls wrapped her in a robe and brought her attention to a tray of jewellery sent in for her, and the security guard beside it. Despite their professionalism, neither masseuse could restrain their giggles – a kind of raw pleasure that scraped against her as she watched them. They nudged her, all girls together, excited. She felt their envy and bewilderment, realised that they were examining her, trying to see what magic she had worked on this man. Where was it – in her pores and crevices, and could they have some, too?

She considered her own feelings as she touched the diamonds. There was a price to be paid, she accepted that. She did not want to think what, but certainly sex. She had never slept with a stranger before; the thought made her feel dull and determined. But she would go with him, and do what he wanted. There was no other ending to the story.

'Your boyfriend says he wants to watch you choose.'

She pulled her robe tight and watched the velvet man come in, through slitted eyes.

★

She had never really kept close friends; the few she did have, from university, and then two colleagues, a man and a woman, all seemed to admire her, but then no more. Jack had been more sociable than she: he had someone over at least once a month to eat the food she cooked and to remark on their flat. Someone had once politely called it a show home, and the praise always left her satisfied.

'Just so,' Jack had said, mimicking her. 'Everything just so. Like you're my fucking mum or something.'

'It doesn't take very much to keep things nice,' she'd argued. 'Just put it back where you found it. Everything in its place. The secret is in the upkeep. Just be organised.'

'I'd like to see you lose your mind, just once,' he said. It was one of the few things he'd ever said with substance; he was no puzzle. But it had surprised her: the force of his wish. Would he have revelled more in her temper or a screaming, undignified orgasm? Or did he want to see her stark staring mad, clawing at the sky?

She'd been glad to see the back of him. Friends of his called to tell her how much they admired her fortitude, her pragmatism; the quiet respect she afforded him during a short period of bitter-mouthed alcoholism, short because well – he was far too judicious to really become a nuisance in anyone's life. He had done his best with her. Just she wore away people, over time. She knew that about herself. She was a transitory experience. Her parents rang infrequently, usually Tuesday, as if they kept a diary somewhere. She was a duty: that was fine.

★

She was shaking by the time they reached her neighbourhood, car inching its way through old buildings like oil. Some arrangement had been made with the market florist and all her pink flowers had been packed carefully, carpeting the floor of the car and overflowing in the back. The driver sneezed. The velvet man stroked her hand. He looked concerned – or was it the grim visage of a man about to claim his pound of flesh? She was horrified. What was the price of this day, of the diamond bracelet on her wrist, its sharp brilliance cutting through the evening gloom?

'Here,' she said. The car slunk into place.

He saw that she was shaking. His face, distressed. 'What can I do?' he said, rubbing and rubbing the back of her thin hand. 'How can I help?' Above them, the balcony of her simple, second-floor apartment loomed.

She turned to face him.

'We have to go somewhere else. I'll do what you say, but not here.'

'I wanted to see your home, full of flowers.'

'Not here,' she hissed. 'No.'

He drew away from her. 'What is it that you think we're going to do?'

She made a gesture, across her body, hand sharp, fingers flailing.

He shook his head, stroked her face.

'You still don't understand. I do what you want. Your pleasure is mine. There is no price.'

She squinted. 'But...'

He laughed, low. Seemed softer than ever.

'Whatever you need.'

She could feel her backbone begin to unfurl. Could there be this kind of man? She didn't know how it worked.

He gathered her face in his hands. 'Anything I can do. It's my pleasure.'

The feeling of recognition returned, that there are spirits that know what you are. She felt something tilt inside. She grasped his shoulders, hurting herself, hurting him, perhaps? It didn't matter. All for her. He said so. An impossibility. Let him see her sins.

★

Her nails bite into his wrist, as they walk towards her front door. There is a nest of silver cobwebs in the eaves, a black garbage bag, strewn in the way. She keeps hold of his hand, fits the key with the other, smoothly opens.

The apartment smells of old washing-up and the cheese of mould. There are pieces of discarded clothing in the hall. They traverse the items, she kicking them out of the way. Old candle wax, long-sputtered across bookshelves. Dust everywhere, on alphabetised books and matching crockery.

She stands, hands dangling, as he takes it in, looking around him, back to her.

There is a half-eaten chicken leg in the middle of the living room floor. The sofa is stained, with matching stained cushions. Detritus teeters: saucers, each sugared with ancient meals. In the kitchen, piles of dirty clothes totter in front of the sink, the full dishwasher, the full washing machine. She has been washing the same clothes for three days, unable to do more than add new liquid, then sit on the dirty kitchen floor, watching the same items wash again, unable to make herself open the door and take the damp items out and spread them on her balcony, or through the flat to dry. Dotted through the rooms are dusters, including a feather one, spray polish, disinfectant, floor-cleaner, bleach. She has been carrying them around, and laying them in piles.

He watches her carefully, nods her on. They are not done.

She has been sleeping on a naked mattress for weeks; it is too much to make the bed at the end of a day. Most of the bed is occupied – half-drunk water bottles among the pillows, hairbands and used tights where she's dragged them off and discarded them. Pills – all her efforts to soothe, improve, heal, take control: Omega-3 supplements, multivitamins, evening primrose oil. A cracked lipstick. There is old vomit down the side of the bed.

The velvet man looks at the flat and looks at her. She is swaying in her shame.

Her mouth cracks open.

'I'm so lonely,' she says.

★

Into the night, she listens: to the scud of a broom across wood; the flushing of a toilet; the tamp-tamp sound of fresh sheets being shaken out; jangling clothes-hangers; a scrubbing brush against the floor, the rattle of pill bottles. Bleach, floor polish. He could pay, but he does it with his hands. Sounds of him lifting the bed, the desk, each one of her shoes. Bags of junk, stink, shame, removed. As dark deepens: the striking of a match for candles and incense; the sweet smell of peonies gathered and fluffed; a choice of low music – guitar and drum, and him, humming along; she begins to breathe again; she dozes; wakes to his lips brushing against her forehead; the snicker of the front door opening and closing.

## ART, FOR FUCK'S SAKE

I had been celibate for a year before a pair of lions happened along. Well, they weren't lions, but the kind of men who make you think of lions, with their tumbling shades of brown and their big soft paws.

I'd decided men were dogs. Panting, impatient things that looked at you with irresistible eyes, then wagged their tails at the very next bitch. When I was fifteen, I met a young man with a mantra. His mother taught it to him: 'There is only one way to handle women. Fool them, fuck them and forget them.' Two can play that game. I'd chosen to forget them. My best friend Marcia fucked them. She specialised in one-night stands where the talking went wrong and the sex went right. But I couldn't imagine a careless grind and a stranger in my bed the next morning. I'd never done anything like that, and I never intended to.

★

I went and sat on Marcia's sofa two hours after I finished my fifth novel. I hadn't seen her for weeks, but she was used to me coming out of post-novel hibernation. That kind of work does things to you, loses you in a world of one. My eyes were bloodshot and my weave needed emergency treatment. Marcia looked at me in friendly disgust.

'Girl,' she said, 'you need some sex.'

'You always think that sex is the answer to everything.'

'Sex is good for you, Simone. You know how much man I check since you disappear into that novel? Me nearly call you the other night to come out, but then me remember you don't business with crotches when you writin'.'

She told me about her latest exploits: a man at a local bar with three golden teeth and an oral technique that made her praise God; another who leaned against her car while she was having her nails done ('The man waited for me two hours!'). I let the details wash over me. Crickets sang through the burglar bars on her living-room window. I loved that sound. Whatever changes in Jamaica, the sound of crickets at night is constant.

The night before I finished the novel, I dreamed crickets and dreamed a man. Just a nice man. Someone who did what he said he would do, and knew that when he touched a woman he made a promise. To cherish her, to love her. To be there. And then we made love: skin and arms and moans among the sounds of crickets calling for a mate. I woke up aching, knowing I'd never find him. There'd been too many lies.

Marcia touched my arm. 'You alright?'

'Yeah. Sorry. That sounds good.'

'You not listening at all.' She laughed and smacked me lightly on the knee. 'Stop pretending.'

I turned to face her. 'Why you make man use you so?'

She screwed up her face. 'I'm not being used.'

'How can you *not* feel used?'

She stretched out for her wineglass and sipped delicately. She looked fragile under the lamp. Perhaps that was why men came to her; maybe they needed to bed something they thought they could break.

'As a writer I would expect more from you,' she said. 'A little more empathy. But never mind that. Somebody's coming over now.'

I stared at her. 'You throwing me out?'

Marcia rolled her eyes. 'Call it whatever you want, girl.'

⋆

Walking back to my car, I thought about how I'd once tried to write a character like Marcia, but couldn't make it work. There were too many things about her motivation that I didn't understand.

She'd forgive me in a day or so, I thought. I felt sorry for her. I'd clearly hit a nerve.

⋆

Two weeks later, in time-honoured middle-class Jamaicanness, my hair was a sleek waterfall down my back and my nails were scarlet. My manuscript was off to my US editor and I was well into what Marcia had dubbed Operation Run Down Man. She was talking to me again, of course she was – just in time for the partying. It wasn't that I never partied. Or flirted. Or laughed. I could do all those things. But I still found myself in the middle of bars and on the front steps of houses sweating into my frock, wondering if everyone could see how dead I felt inside. I didn't want to do this. *Waste of time*, I thought, as men bought me drinks, leered down my cleavage, presented their crotches for me to dance with. Love wasn't this superficial.

It was Joshua who called the next morning as I downed strong coffee and held my head. I grabbed the phone.

'Hello?' I said, hating whoever it was.

'Simone Jacobs?' I had to smile. It was the kind of voice that made you want to smile.

'Yeah, that's me.'

He was very professional. He explained that he was a musician, told me about gigs he'd played and contacts we had in common. A friend introduced him to my novels; now they had a proposal for work.

'Tell me more about the project.' I wasn't curious about the job yet. I just liked how the growl in his voice woke me up.

'We don't have a name for it. We've been calling it Project X.'

Multimedia. He'd do the music; his friend Che would create the central piece, a sculpture. And they wanted me to think about words. A set of short stories, perhaps.

'Is there a theme?' I asked.

'Passion.'

I nearly laughed.

★

I met them in a wine bar off Hope Road. They got to their feet when I entered, like Jamaican men with broughtupcy. I recognised Joshua's voice. He was shorter than Che, but bigger, darker. Barrel chest, rock-faced. Che bounced on his heels, smiling. A yellow man, his hair an explosion of soft, black flames.

We ordered shrimp pasta, bread, crisp salads that weren't. They told me about Project X, interrupting each other, joking, occasionally dropping into the kind of code reserved for old friends. It was nice to watch.

'Blame everything on Che,' said Joshua, mock serious. 'I wanted to explore the implications of twenty-first century post-modernism in Jamaican politics, but *he* wants to get into slack-ness!'

Che bounced, like he couldn't keep still. He coughed over his Red Stripe. '*Me*? You see how you making the woman think is foolishness we trying to do? Passion is everything – not just sex.' His hands were rough, a sculptor's hands. He touched his own face, put his fingers into his mouth, then crossed his arms as if he didn't know what to do with them.

'When did you two first meet?' I asked.

Che rolled his eyes. 'Dis bwoy followed me around school till me talk to him. And I still can't get rid of him.'

Joshua smiled around his wineglass. 'I like your work,' he said to me. 'You care about everything you write.'

'I can't do it unless I care about it.'

'Like playing God, eh?' he said.

'What you mean?'

'You get to make everything turn out right.'

'Well… it's not as simple as that.'

Che patted me on the arm. 'Yeah, man. Of course it is.'

I didn't know very many other artists. I'd never let myself be part of a shared creative space. Novelists are solitary; we might get edited, but we don't like negotiating the rules of the game. Somehow, these two made it look like it would be fun.

Hours went by easily. A vase of flowers wilted on the table. We passed each other cheese and black pepper, much more wine and beer, covering our hands with dying pollen, bright yellow against our palms, sucking pepper shrimp heads. Joshua had longer, more delicate hands, strange on a man of his stature. He knocked things over, but he wasn't clumsy – his energy was just too big for his skin, like it was pouring over the edges of him. They talked to me and each other, showing each other off. They didn't seem to notice the golden pollen cloud across the tablecloth.

'OK,' I said. 'I'll do it.'

They didn't turn me on. They weren't chatting me up. I liked that.

★

We got funding for four months of work. The deadline was non-negotiable, but they reassured me. I was shy, sometimes. They'd worked together before and it took me time to fall into their rhythm. But slowly, I relaxed. For three weeks I went to Che's apartment every Monday, Wednesday and Friday. Fans buzzed overhead. His home was messy: tarps covered works in progress, odd, painful paintings askew on the walls. Too many books to fit, by writers I'd never heard of before, and the fridge smelled bad. I balled up on the edge of a sofa. These day-long sessions took on a life of their own: we bitched, brainstormed, then moved to our own little bubbles of space in the room. I sat scribbling ideas on a pad and then transferring them to my laptop. Joshua played questioning chords, patting a big, fat drum, humming. He was creating sound, but his was still the quietest corner. Che danced around weird buckets and made sketches on pieces of paper. Sometimes there was only the sound of our breathing and our thoughts. It was always Che who got bored first.

One day when I arrived they grabbed me at the door and hauled me back to my car, laughing.

'Give me the keys,' said Joshua.

'You mad? Give you the keys to my *baby*?'

Che snorted and tapped my battered VW bug. 'Look like a big, hardback man to me.'

'Where we going?'

'Manning Cup match.'

'What?'

Joshua tutted. 'Manning *Cup*, woman. You know football, right?'

'Of course, but…'

'JC's playing Campion,' said Che. 'We have to go watch JC bruk up dem rass!'

I rolled my eyes, but I wanted to laugh. 'You guys not over this high school rivalry yet?'

'Never!' they chorused.

★

We wormed our way into bleacher seats; above us, jittering young boys beat drums and cheered before anything had started. People called out to Joshua and Che, so the journey to our seats took a long time, as they swapped stories and memories. They introduced me to everybody; I began to see friends of my own, made my own introductions.

'*JC!*' Che and Joshua yelled as loud as they could. Which was loud. They were both dressed in blue, the colour of their team. Che wrapped an old school tie around his head. He looked ridiculous, and wonderful.

'*Campion!*' roared our rivals.

I watched an old man selling peanuts in the crowd. I hadn't

been to a Manning Cup match for ten years, but I could have sworn it was the same old man who sold me peanuts when I was sixteen. His back was bent into a question mark; the wrinkles that covered his face made an elaborate pattern. I recognised him from the sound of his voice. I'd never been able to understand what he was saying. I plucked at Che's sleeve.

'You know what the peanut man is saying?'

'Who, Burt? He's been here from time.'

'What's he *saying*?'

'You don't have ears?'

I was irritated. 'Che, if I could hear him, I wouldn't have to ask you.'

He reached for my face, closing my eyes under his palms. 'Listen.'

The peanut seller's voice was clear and beautiful under the roars.

'Peee-nuts!' Then that something I couldn't make out. 'Che, I can't…'

'Listen.'

His skin smelled of hot nuts and clay.

'Peeee-nuts! Peee-nuts! If you cyaan crack dem, mumble dem!'

I wanted to giggle. '*Mumble* them?'

Che took his hands away. Pointed at the man. 'See? Him don't have no teeth. If you cyaan crack the peanuts, mumble them. Between your gums.'

We giggled. It was so yardie. I scribbled down a description of the old man as the teams ran onto the pitch and the crowd rose to its feet.

Later, I danced. We all danced, as rhyming insults ran back and forth between supporters of the teams. Our side mashed their rivals into the ground. Someone poured a bottle of beer down the back of my T-shirt and I broke a nail. I didn't care. Che picked me up and put me on his shoulders. I worried that people would complain that they couldn't see, but no one did, so I danced there too.

'Boy, you feel all hot and sweaty,' Che said. Bawled at the field. 'Ref, you *mad* or what?'

I drummed my fists on the top of his head. And when Campion equalised, I prayed, for the first time in a long time. I prayed for the winning goal, and it came, with twenty-five seconds to spare.

★

We worked around each other. We peeled each other's layers. Joshua told me about his divorce three years ago. At some point it became clear that Che had only ever loved one woman in his life. I listened to stories about Joshua's three-year-old boy and his sinus problems. Che insisted on reading Philip K. Dick and Asimov out loud. We listened to Marley and Maxwell's *Urban Hang Suite* and Sade and a little bit of Brahms, Che conducting. But mostly, we worked.

Finally, I let it slip that I was celibate. They thought this was hilarious. They asked me how I was managing. I said it was my choice and nobody else's business. That there were no good men in Jamaica; they were all married or dogs. Or both.

'Is true!' yelled Che. 'Talk it, sister! Man ah dawg!' He hit Joshua. 'You ah dawg?' They howled and barked and I tried to be angry. But I couldn't.

They praised me, like the big brothers I never had. They patted me all the time, on the butt, on my shoulders. They ruffled my hair. They tossed me back and forth between them. I wrote well. Images were fresh, narrative seemed effortless. I said what I meant. One night we got drunk and ate too much pepperoni pizza with pear on top. Joshua and I play-fought with Che's cushions. I was laughing so hard I kept falling down. We ended up on the floor, panting. My legs were plaited through his. They were like iron bars. His face was inches from mine.

'Where *is* your libido, these days?' he asked.

I giggled. 'Nowhere. It took a trip on a sailing ship.'

Che grabbed me by the armpits and slid me out from underneath his friend. '*What* you say you libido doing?'

I blew him a kiss. My head was swimming. I was so rarely silly.

'I hear it's having a nice time in some drunk jungle. But those are only rumours.'

Che shook me. 'So *drunk*. Girl, you need a grind.'

I stuck my tongue out at him. '*Typical* male response.'

'I know what Simone is like in bed…' he teased. The comment was directed at Joshua, like I wasn't there. Joshua smiled indulgently.

'She's the kind of woman who takes hours…' said Che.

I sat cross-legged and swigged some Jack. 'You don't know *nothing*!'

'She's not the kind of woman you can check for five minutes,' said Che. 'She likes a lot of foreplay –'

'*Every* woman likes that.'

He ignored me. 'Kind of woman who'd cover you in scented oil, rub you down, feed you. Take a bath, suck you, back off again. Tease.'

Inside me, something was turning over and burning. He wasn't talking about the way I was: just how I'd always planned to be. If someone loved me, I could be that way.

'She'd want to drive you crazy, keep you waiting. And just when you can't take anymore, she lets you in. And then you just settle *down* into the pum-pum.' He sighed, theatrically.

We laughed. I laughed because I was embarrassed. I didn't know why Joshua was laughing, but I did know his knee was brushing mine. It was a small thing; it might even have been an accident. He had one hand around the stem of his beer bottle, rubbing it up and down. The movement of his hand seemed languorous, lazy but purposeful. I stared at the hand, trying to remember what it reminded me of. I could suddenly imagine what he'd looked like as a boy. I wanted to tell him everything was alright.

'What?' he asked.

'Nothing,' I said.

Teasing over, Che went back to his work, body set in concentration. He was moulding a woman's hips from what looked like play dough. In the background, Joshua got to work with the Rizlas. I wrote. Drunk. Regardless. Squiggles all over the page like a kid.

★

And then one night I got to the house and found Joshua prowling around the door, banging. He looked as if he wanted to cry and I felt suddenly sick.

'What *is* it?' My heart was beating too fast.

'Che won't answer the door.'

'So maybe he's not there.'

He glared at me. 'He's *there*.' He pounded. 'Che! Answer the bloodclaaht door!'

Silence.

'Joshua, what is the matter?'

'Him sick, alright?'

'What you mean?'

He pounded again.

'*Joshua!*'

There was a slight crack of the door and we could see Che's face.

He was nearly unrecognisable. From yesterday. His hair had gone dull. His eyes were dull. Joshua put a foot in the crack and shoved. Che scuttled back and sat in a corner.

Later, I tried to tell Marcia about this most passionate of men, swollen with bleakness, scratches on his face and his hands where he'd been trying to distract himself. I never knew that the one woman Che loved, had died. Stabbed with an ice pick on a bus. For a gold chain and a near-empty purse.

'So what did you do?' Marcia asked.

'Me? Nothing. It was Joshua talking to him. He put him to bed. He's still there now. He says this happens every couple months. He's manic depressive.'

She frowned. 'But the man have to get over this, girl. Is how long since him woman dead?'

'Three years.'

'Isn't that when Joshua wife lef' him?'

'Yeah. They brought each other through.'

'Rahtid.' She hugged me. 'Simone, I love you. But if my man dead, and your marriage mash up, I don't know whether I can do one damn thing fi you.'

I tried to smile. 'So you planning to give up you slack ways and get a man?'

'If you can find me one like dem two. But not the mad one.'

'*Marcia!*'

'Just jokin', baby.'

We hugged.

'I'm scared,' I said.

'What now?'

'I want him to be better.'

'And...?'

I buried my face in her shoulder. I felt so guilty. 'I want us to *finish*.'

'But you can always publish the stuff you're doing now –'

'No. That's not how it works. It's *ours*. It has to be all of us.'

★

Three days passed. I knew I should have tried to help, but I couldn't think how. And then Che arrived on my doorstep, carrying a bucket. I hugged him at the door and gave him lemonade. I was awkward. I didn't know what to say, but his bounce was back, small, but present.

'So how you feel?' he asked.

'Me? How *you* feel?'

He looked around my apartment. 'This place is just like you.'

I sighed inwardly. Cream and orderly, just like my mother would have liked it. Sometimes I wanted to be untidy, but I couldn't.

'No it isn't,' I said.

He smiled. 'But it is, y' know. Not the fancy sofa or the colour, but look.' He got up and moved around, touching things. A bottle of oil on the side table. He opened it and sniffed. 'I can smell it in your hair.' He brushed the wind chimes at the window with his palm. 'You play with these when you're lonely. And –' he sat on the sofa again and reached underneath. I watched him, disbelieving, as he pulled out a sheaf of paper. 'Yeah man, me did know. You sit here writing bad poetry. All about man, right? Man that leave you.'

'Shut *up!*' I snatched the paper.

'Do me a favour. Give me your hand.'

'What?'

'Your writing hand.'

He covered my left hand in something that felt like Vaseline. His touch was quiet and efficient; I stayed quiet and let him rub the jelly into each crease and crevice, up to my forearm. He pushed the bucket forward. 'Stick your hand in this. It's plaster.'

I obeyed. We were quiet again. After a while he signalled for me to pull out of the bucket. After the cast dried, he pulled it off me. We regarded the disembodied hand in silence. Its fingers were spread, long, frozen in a caress. He placed the hand on my side table. I didn't know my hand looked like that. Capable. Powerful.

'That's for you,' he said. 'I'll finish it and then you can have it.'

We'd never worked anywhere else but his house, but I could see that wasn't right anymore: he'd exposed too much. We ordered pizza and called Joshua. I knew they'd move the sofa and disturb my neighbours; I decided not to care. We'd begun again.

★

I gave them just over thirty thousand words and then I didn't see them for weeks. They said they wanted to surprise me, but I was vex as hell. It was strangely unbearable. I prowled my house. I kept on writing, astonished that another novel was coming, with two protagonists. One with dishevelled hair and sad eyes, one with skin like jet rock. But there was space for other things too. More balance. I masturbated idly, called old friends. I was writing, not hiding. A new way.

'Not even *one* of them did make a move?' asked Marcia.

'Don't be stupid.'

She ignored me. 'Which one you prefer?'

'It's not like that.' My head hurt. 'Neither.'

'I woulda grab at least *one* grind offa them,' she said, grimly.

'Yes, I know.'

I felt sour about her all over again.

Dreamt once about golden pollen spilling across the table-cloth, and hands.

★

They call me, finally. It's finished.

The drive takes so long.

Joshua meets me at the door. If he were Che, he would be dancing from one foot to the other. Because he is Joshua, he is still and mysterious. He carries a blindfold.

'May I?' he says.

I let him tie me blind. I let him put a hand in the small of my back, another on my shoulder. I let him guide me.

In the room, there is silence, and then the sound of drums. I want to reach for the sound, to grab it, to pull it to me. It is sound that could be felt, that could be loved. It is just like Joshua: solid, unmistakable. But there is a new vibe, something I didn't know he was feeling. The sound of mischief conquering rationality. It is a gorgeous surrender of his masks. I pull back against him. 'It's beautiful, Joshua.'

'Of course it is. It would have to be.'

'You so full of yourself.'

He laughs. 'You don't understand. Listen.'

I listen. Then I realise. It's not just him. There's a dark piano chord for Che.

'It's us,' I breathe.

'Yes,' he says. 'But with you at the centre. Hear it?'

A guitar wails through.

I want to cry. 'That's me?'

'If you were sound, yeah.'

And I know what they have done. 'Let me see the sculpture.'
He unties the blindfold and light creeps into the room. Trickles of blue smoke. I stare.

The sculpture reaches almost to the ceiling. Che has crafted her of apricot soapstone. My stories climb across her skin and flood onto the wall behind her, the ground beneath her, in oranges, yellows, reds, against the blue. The sculpture's eyes are blurred and beautiful, as if she is looking at forever. She is naked. Hands soft in her lap. Fingers wreathed in golden pollen. She's not me; that would be too much. But she's something we all know.

★

I think it will be Che, with his whip-efficient body, coming from behind the sculpture, dancing up to us, so proud. I am wet-eyed. But it's Joshua who brings it to a beginning.

'Look at how beautiful you are,' he says.

He puts his hand between my legs, and I realise that more than my eyes are wet. I am amazed that what he does is OK, that a kiss was not what I needed first. He is stroking me through my thin leggings, and his hand knows me. I don't think of protest, of the future, even how it will be right this minute. I just sink into Joshua as Che stands behind me, waiting his turn.

Joshua is slow. Slower than I ever could have imagined. The drums have not stopped, and he winds the music through my hair. His breath is hot. I'm moaning their names like a string of moonstones, like their names make one name.

Joshua gives me to Che. He sits on the floor and watches his friend pull my blouse over my head. I watch him watching us. Che picks me up, leans against the wall, pulls my legs around his waist, my heels in the small of his back. He pulls off his shirt, lifts my breasts until our nipples are touching. I look into his face, so serious.

'You're a clever man,' I say. My throat hurts. He buries his face into my neck. The rub of his skin against mine makes me want to scream. He is rubbing me into him, masturbating me against his waist and groin. His legs are trembling with the effort. I look back at Joshua. He is naked, has his dick in his hand, rubbing and rubbing. I want it in my mouth. I slide off Che, kneel in front of Joshua, run my tongue around his balls, tickle the underside, listen to him groan.

We have no co-ordination. It doesn't matter. It's play. We're purring. Cleaning whiskers. They pull my panties off, ripping fabric. We are all laughing like children. Tails wave in the air. I am on the floor, blue music and blue smoke and blue arms cradling me in the queer light. Joshua spreads my legs and dips his head into me, licking me thoughtfully. I push my hips into his face. He slips his fingers inside me and rubs the moisture across my lips. Che leans over me, sucking my mouth. He groans against my cheek. He is naked too. His cock is shorter than Joshua's, but thicker, and he pushes his erection away from his belly again and again, an odd urgency. I reach for him, wanting to feel him, but he pins my hands back to the floor.

'You work too hard,' he whispers into my hair.

I can't disagree; I can't concentrate. Joshua's tongue is so thick, inside me, up and down my thighs. I want to grab his head and fuck his mouth, but I can't move. Che is kissing me upside down, his teeth are in my neck, his paws spread on mine. I am leaping up the rungs of a ladder, pussy wetter and wetter.

'Tell him to suck me,' I beg.

'Suck her…' Che whispers to his friend.

Joshua groans into my crotch. He is tossing his head side to side. No one has eaten me like this before. I'm up the ladder. I am at the top of the fucking ladder, I am falling over the ladder.

They have no mercy. None at all. I cum in Joshua's mouth and minutes later Che is over me, sliding into me, one sure movement, *bam*, like a fireball. I cling to his back as he rides me, I can feel them turning me, like a sculpture. I am riding him now, just slow and easy. I can feel liquid clay dripping down me, down the crack of my ass, and I know what Joshua means to do. My shoulders freeze.

'Let me,' he breathes against my neck.

'But... but...' I have an absurd fear about cleanliness. Did I wash properly? Do I smell good? Che is bucking inside me, throbbing.

'Just let me, Simone...' Joshua murmurs. 'Stop thinking.'

I push my ass back into him and he begins to slide into me. I breathe. I think good thoughts, hot thoughts. I will myself to relax, as more inches invade me.

Che stops, abruptly. He grabs my hips, makes me stop. Confused, frustrated, I look down into his face. Joshua has stopped too. Fear swirls in me. They are regretting it, regretting me.

Then I understand.

They can feel each other. There is only a thin layer of me between them, and a strange kind of confusion in Che's eyes. I wait. I cannot bear the moment; my body is crying for movement. But I wait. They have never thought of going this far, and because of this, they are afraid. Of what it shows them. Of what it shows me.

Che lets go of my hips and spreads his hands away from the sides of his body. Joshua's hands are on my shoulders. We are all very still. The music has stopped. There is only the sound of us breathing.

Joshua's hand slides down to the floor as Che's hand comes up towards it. They touch palms, fingers lingering.

I watch, fascinated. It is so brief.

Che pushes up inside me, just a small movement. My pussy grabs him, hard.

Joshua sighs. 'You like what he's doing to you?'

'Oh yes...' I moan.

Joshua pulls his penis out of me, halfway out. Then back into me again, so slowly, so gently, I can only gulp air.

Che smiles up at me as his friend sinks home.

'You like how he feels?' he says.

And they're fine.

They double-fuck me as if they have been doing it all their lives. In the minutes it takes, in the strange hours it takes, in the years that we all fuck and love each other, it feels as if a million hands are in my hair, a thousand lips on my skin. I am speaking in tongues, to the slap of thighs, I am calling out that old plea, the only thing right in this moment. I give in. I demand.

'Fuck me, fuck me, *fuck* me!' I say.

And in some part of them, they fuck each other too.

★

They dress me in the blue light, stroking every pubic hair into place, pulling my panties up my legs, scattering kisses along my back as they hook my bra, smoothing my skin, soothing my ass.

We sit on the floor, look at Project X and smile at each other. They are not dogs. They are lions. I hold up my head in the face of their grace and their beauty. I can't wait to tell Marcia.

For I am a lion, too.

'Art,' I say.

We hold hands, all of us.

## THE WOMAN WHO LIVED
## IN A RESTAURANT

One high day in February, a woman walks into a two-tier restaurant on a corner of her busy neighbourhood, sits down at the worst table – the one with the blind spot, a few feet too close to the kitchen's swinging door – and stays there.

She stays there forever.

She wears a crisp cotton white shirt with a good collar and cuffs and a soft black skirt that can be hiked up easy. She has careful dreadlocks strung with silver beads – the best hairstyle to take into forever. There is no more jewellery; her skin is naked and moist. She keeps a tiny pair of white socks in her handbag and, in the cold months, she slips them onto her bare feet.

She watches the waiters, puppeting to and fro, the muscles in their asses tightening and relaxing, thumbing coin and paper tips, tumbling up and down the stairs and past her to the kitchen, careful not to touch. The maître d' has a big belly and so does the chef, who is also the owner of the restaurant. Nobody holds it against them; they work very long hours and the chef's food is extremely fine; this is not fat, it is gravitas.

'Smile, smile,' the maître d' says to everybody, staff and customers alike; he has been here the longest and she never hears him say much more in front of house, although you would have thought he might.

She goes to the restroom in the mornings and evenings, to

wash her skin and to put elegant slivers of fresh oatmeal soap to her throat and armpits. She nods at the diners, who bring children and lovers and have arguments and complain and compliment the food – and some get drunk, and then there's the sound of vomiting from the bathroom that makes her wince. So many come to propose marriage she can spot them on sight: the men lick their lips and brandish their moustaches and crunch their balls in their hands. They all flourish the ring in the same way, like waiters setting down the *pièce de résistance* – fresh steak tartare or twisted sugar confections that attract the light. Their women – provided they are pleased – do identical neck rolls and shoulder raises and matching squeals. Like a set of jewellery she thinks, all shining eyes, although one year a woman became very angry and crushed her good glass into the table top.

'I told you not to kill it with this lovey-dovey shit!' she yelled at the moustachioed man, and stalked out. The man sat with the napkin under his chin, making a soft, white beard. The napkins are of very good quality.

'Hush,' said the restaurant woman, like she was rocking the small pieces of the leftover man. The people around them ate on, and tried to ignore the embarrassed, shattered glass.

'What shall I do?' he asked, rubbing his mouth with the napkin.

'Love is what it is.' She stretched one finger skyward, as if offering an architectural suggestion.

He hurried out, his shoes making scuffling noises, like mice.

*

These days she must rock from cheek to cheek to prevent sores. But mostly she sits and waits and smiles to herself and her lips remind the male waiters of the entrails of a plum, so juicy and broken open. They see that she is not young, although she has good breasts and healthy breath. Watch how she taps her fingers on the table and handles the glass stem, they whisper. This is a woman of authority. She has been somebody. Some of the waitresses weep, but most of them hiss that she is a fool.

'Mind the chef kill you,' the line cook whispers.

One waitress deliberately spills fragrant, scalding Jamaican coffee onto the woman's wrist. The woman rubs her burned flesh and smiles. The waitress shudders at her happy brown eyes.

'Stupid bitch,' the waitress hisses. 'Why are you *here*?'

She is fired the next day, as are all waitresses who hate the woman.

★

A young male waiter fills the vacancy – three years and thirteen hours after the woman arrived to live in the restaurant. She sees him come in for the interview, nervous with his thick curly hair and handsome bow legs.

On his first day, the waiter comes running to the pass to say that he has seen a woman bathing in the restroom sink, and that her body was long and honeyed and gleaming in the early light coming through the back window. He didn't mean to see her, really, he says. He was dying for a piss and opened the wrong door.

What he does not say is this. That when he opened the door, the woman was sitting naked, with her shoulder blades propped up against the wall between the cubicles. Her legs were spread so far apart that the muscles inside her thighs were jumping. She had the prettiest pussy he's ever seen, so perpendicular and soft that he had to shade his eyes and take a breath, and then, without knowing he was capable of such a thing, he stopped and stared.

'Put simply,' he says to his closest friend, that night, while drinking good beer and wine, 'she was too far gone to stop.'

They sigh, together.

The woman, who had been rolling her nipples between her fingers before he came in, put a hand between her legs. At first he thought she was covering herself, but then he saw the expression on her face and realised that this was a lust he'd never seen before. The woman took her second and third fingers and rubbed between her legs so fast and hard that the waiter, who thought he'd seen a woman orgasm before this, suddenly doubted himself and kept watching to make sure. In the dawn, the woman's locks could have been on fire and even the shining tiles on the bathroom floor seemed to ululate to help her.

'Ah,' said the woman. 'Oh.'

The smallest sound, so quiet. It was like a mouthful of truffle or a perfect pomegranate seed on the tongue: of an unmistakeable quality.

★

Weeks pass, and the new waiter is miserable, not least because he knows now that he has never made a woman orgasm.

'What is she doing here, hardly ever moving from her seat? Does she not have a home?'

'Mind the chef kill you,' they whisper around him.

Despite their warnings he rages on, making the soup too peppery and the napkins rough.

Finally, the maître d' tells him the story, in between cold glasses of water, changing tarnished forks and cutting children's potato cakes into four pieces each. All through it, the waiter tries not to look at the woman under his eyelashes, although when he does, she still glows and when the chef sends her an edible flower salad for her luncheon, he can still smell the salt on her second and third fingers when he puts it down in front of her.

The maître d' explains that the story is in the menus, if you read them closely enough.

The chef is the kind of man who is in love with his work. He has owned the restaurant for twenty-two years and it is everything. He creates ever more beautiful and tasty dishes; he admires the beams and wall fixtures and runs loving fingers over the icy water jugs and bunches of fresh beans in the kitchen. The mushrooms are cleaned with a specially crafted brush. Hours must be spent on the streets and in markets talking with butchers and local fishermen so that the restaurant has the freshest, most rare ingredients. Each tile in the floor has been hand-painted. Each window-sash handmade. He has been known to stroke the carpet on the stairs, and he knows the name and taste buds of every regular customer.

He is a happy and most successful man.

But then he met the gleaming, honeyed woman in a farmers' market. She was buying a creamy goat's cheese and several wild mangoes, and he wasn't ever able to say why, but he stopped to talk and point out the various colours of the dying sun above the market. The gathering day drew purple shadows over the woman, like bruises, and he liked her very much indeed. He thought there was something missing from his life, and that he could get it from her.

At first the chef did not worry, says the maître d' to the young waiter. He knew that he could love, because he loved the restaurant, and though some might say one cannot love a restaurant the way one loves a woman, both take time and attention, so there we are.

'There we are, where?' snaps the waiter. 'We are not anywhere. Why is that woman sitting there for years?'

'You understand nothing,' says the maître d'. 'You should wait for the rest of the story.'

The chef, says the maître d, prepared for change. He would do so-and-so at a different time, so he would be able to kiss the woman. And this or that ingredient – well, after he and the woman became lovers, he would not be able to rise quite so early to collect it, so they would have to make do with another version of the dish. And so on. The chef brought the woman to see the restaurant and she sat on its couches and chairs, and admired its warm stoves and brightly coloured walls. She brought several good and mildly expensive paintings, as obeisance, and very good flowers – bird of paradise and cross-breed orchids – and lovingly arranged them in bowls. But even then, it seemed, she knew something. She stayed out of the kitchen when the chef was busy, even when he smiled and called her in.

'The steam will play havoc with my hair, darling,' she said, for these were the days when she hot-comb straightened it.

'We all knew it was coming, of course,' says the maître d', signalling for the boys to peel the potatoes louder and to bang the pots, so that the chef cannot hear his gossiping. 'We all knew, for after all, which sensible man introduces his girlfriend to his wife?'

Three months after meeting, the sweethearts decided to consummate their affair. On that fated night of intention, the woman arrived for dinner and stayed until one am, which was as early as the chef would close. The staff waited to be dismissed, glad for a break and glad for the lovers. The chef tried to stop looking like a cat with several litres of fresh cream – and tried to stop sweating. The woman, ah, so sweet she was, nervous and happy. They were transformed in their anticipation of the lovemaking, like young things, though neither of them young.

They were leaving through the front door when the restaurant moved two inches to the right.

'That's correct. We all felt it, standing there,' says the maître d'. 'It is hard to explain, even today, and the architect who came to see the torn window frames and the shattered tiles said it was an earthquake, albeit a very localised and small one. Electrics twisted, stove mashed, water from burst pipes running down the coral dining room walls. They opened the crooked fridges and out belched rotted fish and fowl, blackened, sweet with ruin, filling the air, making them all choke. So much money lost! Smile, smile, I told them all, but the sound! The plumbers said it was the pipes, and the electrician, she said it was the wiring, but no one knew, except us. The restaurant would not be left on its own, so it was crying.'

'Will you not kiss me,' said the woman, tugging at the chef, but no, he was unable.

'We could go far away from here,' she begged, but he looked at her as if she was mad.

'I would not hurt her,' he said, almost stern.

'A restaurant?' she said, and she tried to fit all her pain into those two words.

'It is a good restaurant,' he said. And turned back to work.

The newly hired waiter interrupted the maître d'. He was almost stuttering in his outrage.

'So-so-so –?'

The maître d' pulled a pig haunch close to him and began to burn the bristles on the hot stove. It was not his job, but he liked doing it.

'So, the woman came to live here,' he continued. 'She stays here so that she can see the chef, and the restaurant keeps watch.'

'But-but…'

'They sit together, between service, and talk. They do not touch.' The maître d' smiled, almost sadly, tossing the hot pig from palm to palm. He shrugged towards the restroom. 'We have seen her too, my friend. It must be terribly frustrating.'

★

The woman becomes aware that something has changed. Truly, she has seen staff appalled before this. Seen them lounging around her, trying to get her attention. But this young waiter seems more determined, in the way of youth, and he keeps touching her.

'Will you not come to the front door with me?' he says, over her porridge breakfast, sent out strictly at 9.31 am. 'There are pink blooms all over the front of the restaurant, and ivy, and it is so very good.'

'You can describe it for me,' she says, smiling and ripping her languid eyes away. There is lavender, sprinkled in an intricate pattern, on top of her porridge.

The next day: 'Come for a walk with me upstairs,' he says. 'To the balcony. It will be good for you to have the air. The chef' – she moves her shoulders in delight at the sound of his name and slices into the waiter's heart – 'the chef, he has gone out to buy vegetables.'

'I know,' she says. 'He tells me everything that he does. But I'll stay here. It will be better.'

'Better than what?'

She laughs, shifts, pats his shoulder.

'Better than missing his return,' she says, as if he is a stupid child. She gestures to the front door, which is clear because it is too early for the madness of diners. 'I will see him with the sun against his back, and he assures me that from that distance, he can see the purple shadows on me. It will give us much pleasure.'

★

One afternoon, the waiter can control himself no longer. He pulls the woman to her feet, feeling her burning skin beneath his fingers. He is surprised to find the chef suddenly there, standing between them, belly glaring, his best knife tucked behind him. The waiter need say nothing more; his job, perhaps his life, is in jeopardy.

But still he thinks of her. At night, he pulls himself raw. He thinks of her over and above him, and in time the fantasies become vile and violent things. In his desperation he can think of nothing but defiling her, mashing her lips against the wall of his bedroom. He becomes a whisperer, appals himself by hissing at her, like others before him. At first she cannot hear him when he mutters under his breath.

'Stupid bitch,' he says. 'Stupid fucking bitch.' But soon he cares less, and says it when he passes her as he's sweeping, and as he puts filo pastry, with fresh bananas, passion fruit sauce and black pepper ice cream in front of her. 'Stupid bitch, I hope it makes you fat and ugly.'

She looks away, smiling into the distance.

A diner complains.

'Each time I come here, that woman is served something exquisite, off menu. Last week it was out-of-season cherries with kirsch. Last month it was an upside down tomato tart with olive sugar. Why does the chef show such favouritism?'

The young waiter rushes over. 'Madame, that is because she is a stupid bitch, and he is a cruel bastard.'

'Oh my,' says the disgruntled diner.

That evening, the waiter is fired. Before he leaves, he pisses in the fish stew on the stove, throws out a batch of very expensive hybrid vodka and flashes his cock at the calm and waiting woman sitting at the table. She is circling her wrists and pointing her pretty toes under the tablecloth. Her backbone makes a crackling noise.

'What are you waiting for?' he screams at her, as sous chef and maître d' wrestle him out. 'What are you waiting for him to *give* you?'

She answers him, but there is a noise in the walls of the restaurant and so he cannot hear what she says.

★

In the lateness of the night, she rises from the table. After these many years, she has become attuned to the restaurant, and to her beloved. She can hear the eaves sigh in the wind, feel the dining-room chairs sag with relief as the frenetic energy of the day finally draws to a close.

She pushes open the door to the kitchen and steps in, light.

The chef is slumped over a stained steel surface, tired, a good wine at his head. He looks up and smiles at her. It is the best part of his day. The love of the restaurant around him, and now, this sweet woman. She leans on the work surface and faces him, smiling back.

He remembers her complaining, wailing friends. One tried to get the restaurant shut down. Another threatened arson. Her brother, he was the worst. He came to the chef's home, and begged.

'If she does this, my friend, she will give up everything. Home. Job. The chance of children. And worst of all, she will be second best. You make her second best.'

'I know,' the chef said. 'But she is stubborn.'

He has learned to live with guilt. Some days, he thinks it is harder for him. So many of the staff become angry, especially the women. To love them both is tiring. But he has come to respect the woman's choice.

He groans, content, as she steps behind him, puts her arms around him, nestles into the sensitive skin of his neck.

'Hello, my love,' she says.

He reaches behind him, hooks his hands at the small of her back. They look up, towards the ceiling, as if making architectural decisions.

'Has anything changed?' she asks, as she has every night, for years.

They listen to the restaurant, creaking and warm.

'No,' he sighs.

'Ah then,' she says. 'Perhaps, tomorrow.'

They kiss.

It is the same as it always is, except it seems to them both that the kiss deepens and ripens, year on year. First he kisses her eyelids, brushing his lips over lashes and the small wrinkles beginning to sprout nearby. He swallows her breath, and she his. They lick each other like small animals at their mother's hide, nipping, careful, so they do not hurt, or encourage fire. They are slow and careful and respectful, listening to the room around them. He can taste her smile on his lips. She can feel the change in his body, the way his skin thickens when she touches him, the shrug of his shoulders as he controls himself, again. She thinks that if there is one single night when his wanting is gone, she will leave this place – if there is one night when his shoulders flatten and the kiss is the kiss of a brother.

He makes a small, grunting noise against her lips.

'Ah.'

So quiet.

She can feel the kick of his penis against his belly, and the love in his fingertips, as he pulls his face away and kisses her fingers.

She is happy.

Few, she finds, understand.

★

The woman who lives in the restaurant stays there until her hair turns grey and her muscles soften. The chef dies at home, in his bed, thinking of her and of his restaurant. A week later, the maître d' finds her still and cooling body, her head on the soft white cloth of the table, and thinks again, as he often has done, about slicing off her still-juicy lips and sautéing them in butter to make a pie. He tries to move her body, but finds that her atrophied feet are welded to the floor. He yanks and tugs, calls for help, and several men pull and push, saying, 'Well now, be careful, respect to the lady dead' and all that, but there is no success. Eventually they stop when the restaurant begins to creak and to roll dangerously, like a ship listing on a bad sea.

By the time the maître d' returns with an undertaker and a pickaxe, the woman's feet have become tile like the floor; her body is no longer flesh but velvet, and her eyes are glass beads. In fact, as the maître d' looks on, he sees that the woman has become nothing more than an expensive dining chair, pulled up to the table, and perfect for it.

'Love,' grunts the maître d'. He is very old. He taps the restaurant walls and leaves them to it.

## SMILE

They meet and say things; ornate kisses; she feasts on the corner of his mouth. 'Hush,' she says, and his shoulders unpeel. He does what he says he'll do: call, email, arrive. It makes her friends jealous. He feeds her avocado rolls. She goes without make-up and sleeveless, because she feels beautiful. He's glad she listens to him. He resurrects ambitions.

It's not too late, they think, to be happy.

One Thursday, he shows her his red erection; they're not lovers yet and she laughs: 'What are you doing?' He wants to share all his feelings. When he was small, his father nailed a smile to his face: 'It makes your mother happy, son.' So now he smiles, regardless.

'I think we'll do forever,' he says.

'You can't say that,' she says.

She's waited on forever, forever, but now she's frightened she won't get it.

Thirteen months hurry, hurry hurry past and then he leaves her. Not for want of love, but because they hurry hurry hurry. He shows her the tears on his smiling lips before he goes.

★

Her chest stops; she's used to him; there are no colours. The sound of things is like booming. She finds the heart of a steer but it makes her pant. The heart of a wise man floats outside her dress and bleeds on her shoes.

'Jesus,' she says and lies on someone's floor.

Cats come and sniff.

If his mother was still alive she would say: 'You can stop now, son; stop smiling.'

## COVENANT

Have you turned the tape recorder on yet? Maybe you should let me collect my thoughts first. This might be one of your harder debriefing sessions.

I'm not saying I don't want to tell you; this is one of the reasons I came to the Covenant. I like the idea of sharing in this way. It brings us all closer together. I just don't know where to start.

OK. Wherever I like?

OK.

It was easy to leave Abe, in the end – after turning it over so many times in my mind. I wasn't happy. I wanted more. I did try. For nearly ten years. Straight out of my father's house, into Abe's arms.

I haven't thought about my father for a while. But mornings like this, they make me think of home. So clear and silent. I'd wake Daddy up so he could get me ready for school. All the men in my life sleep hard. I've set out Abe's clothes for a business meeting, I've read books with my bedside lamp blaring in his face, I've walked up and down the bedroom with Zak teething and wailing, and that man kept right on – itching, fidgeting, farting and sleeping. About a month ago I lay beside him and stuck him with a pin. It slid in like butter. I tried different parts of his body, near to the bone, through his belly, deeper each time. He just flapped at me like I was a fly. Didn't open his eyes. I did it for ten minutes. He was covered with tiny pools of blood. I lay there and I thought, *Boy, you could sleep for Jamaica.*

I didn't do a lot of sleeping in those last weeks before I left. I sat up and did crochet. Baskets and blankets. The darkness meant I didn't have to pretend I was okay. Two o' clock in the morning made the bruises on my hands fade away. It was so quiet, just the noise of cars in the distance. I pretended I could hear my neighbours in bed, breathing. In their perfect existences.

Mamma painted my room pink before she left; that's what my father told me. Then, when she was gone, there were pink sheets, an army of Barbies and a birthday party every year. Bouncy castles and jugglers. Bottles of perfume, a diamante choker, a golden diary with a matching pen, high-heeled shoes. When I got older, the boys had to come into the front room and sit on the mahogany sofa and state their intentions.

When I was eight, me and Mary-Anne Teddington snapped the heads off all my Barbies. I think we wanted to see what was inside. We cut off their hair and laid them out in a row on the bed, admiring them. My father came in and started to shout, 'You know how much dem tings cost?' He cussed out Mary-Anne until she bawled, and he told her mother she couldn't play with me anymore. Then he took me on his lap and hushed me. Said he knew his little girl wouldn't ever break the dolls he bought her. When he put me to bed, I couldn't sleep. I kept seeing Mary-Anne's big brown eyes fill with tears. I fell asleep, looking at the doll hair in the wastepaper basket.

Golden curls.

Sorry, I'm rambling. Is this the kind of detail you want to hear?

I told you, leaving was simple. I went into Zak's room, and I stood there for a bit, looking at the moons and stars on his bedroom ceiling. Abe painted them with a special fluorescent light you can see in the dark. He painted waves around the edge of the walls. He could be kind, even with all that hand-to-hand combat.

I woke Zak up. He rolled over and looked at me with his face full of sleep. Eyes like wet river stones. He let me dress him, not a whimper. His cheek was warm against my face, leaning against me, still dozing. Just like his father. He asked me, 'Mamma, whatcha doin?' and I said, 'We're going on an adventure, baby.' His face was speckled with those moons and stars.

He went to sleep again in the back of the car. I was worried that he'd roll off the seat when I reversed, but he didn't. He just lay there, sucking his thumb. Abe doesn't like the suck-thumb business. He used to slap Zak's wrist, not hard. Told me that if we were still in Jamaica he would get aloe vera and smear it on Zak's fingers. You ever see fresh aloe vera? No, I guess you haven't. Anyway, it tastes metallic, really bad.

A couple of hours later I was driving down the A20 thinking that doing it at night isn't so scary, especially when you're driving towards freedom. The road was well lit, and you signposted really well. Every few miles that little red arrow and THE COVENANT. I've appreciated all your support, how you knew I'd be coming a long way, and at night, with a child. When you told me on the phone that you'd booked us into a hotel, I was really pleased. Did you know I was getting choked up? You didn't, did you? I'm very good at hiding my feelings. It's been essential.

Cars passed us sometimes. My hands had stopped shaking, and I was desperate for a smoke, but it was too cold to crack a window, and I didn't want to fill the car with fumes. Zak frowns at me when I smoke. Like his daddy.

My father didn't believe that little girls should run. Or be untidy. So I joined the track team. My father didn't believe that little girls should smell bad, so I didn't brush my teeth for days. I stank through half of third form until the personal development programme teacher took me into the nurse's office and pressed a gift pack on me. Deodorant and soap and body spray and tooth-paste. I went into the school bathroom afterwards and rubbed my sanitary pads on the walls. The streaks went brown across the graffiti. Obliterated all the Susanne-heart-Bobbies and the I-love-Adrians.

We got to the Holiday Inn and the receptionist lowered her voice when she saw Zak snoring in my arms. She buzzed a boy to take the luggage, and we got into the elevator and watched the lights on the panel run up, one, two, three, fourth floor. I was near to dropping when we got to the room. The boy helped me put Zak on the bed, and we stood there and watched him, spit leaking out of the side of his mouth onto the pillow. The bag boy grinned and told me he was a lovely lad. 'He looks just like you,' he told me, heading out the door. Everybody says that.

★

Having Zak was Abe's idea, but I was desperate enough to agree. *Normal, normal, normal*, I kept thinking. *Give up the dreams, Sarah and deal with reality*. Being who I really was, that was out of the question. Easier to be a good girl. The punches and the screams were less complicated.

Hagar was less complicated.

She sat there in my living room, wiggling her dirty toes in her housework slippers. She had perfect young skin, even with a spray of acne on her left cheek. We told her that there was nothing wrong with Abe's sperm; just me, barren, empty. Abe was trying to go on like it was a small thing while he was talking; I guess he was trying to make me feel better. When we were done, the little bitch just sat there, wiggling her toes, looking confused.

'So… Missa Abe, me an' you…?' she said.

He cleared his throat. I looked at her toes, and she looked at her toes. Abe laughed. He was like a little pickney in a toy store, and I wondered whether he was enjoying it. He put a hand on her shoulder. I sat there thinking, you should be touching my shoulder. And he said, 'No, no, Hagar. Not at all like that. I'll provide you with the um…'

She didn't say anything, but there was a little smile on her face.

Abe tried again: 'You know, Hagar. I will… um… get some of my… and give it to you, and what you need to do is…' Then he looked at me. *Woman's business*, I could hear him thinking. So I said, 'Hagar, what me and Mr Abe want you to do is take some of his *spirit*, you know, spirit? And put it inside your body, in your privates. It has to be a special time. When do you see your monthlies?'

She giggled, with her bleeding, fertile self. I thought maybe I was being unfair. She was young and ignorant and it was we who were taking advantage of her, after all. That was when she looked up straight into my husband's face, like I wasn't there. Confident as anything.

'I can only do it God way,' she said. We stared at her. I don't think Abe knew what she meant right away, but I knew exactly what the bitch wanted. 'If you want it, me have to do it *God* way.'

Abe is a handsome man, but she never had to make it so obvious. I sat there thinking, *she thinks she can have him. She thinks she can tie him to her, with her tight body.*

He looked at me. I gritted my teeth and told him I'd think about it.

★

I sat on that hotel bed that night and wondered about coming here, and what it would feel like to do everything I wanted to do. Normal isn't the same for everybody. I started to grin, then chuckle, then before I knew it I was muffling the sound of my laughter in the pillow, so I wouldn't wake Zak up. I lay there with my whole body shaking… joyous. So thankful for the Covenant. So thankful for *you*, and the morning you came to my house, like an inside-out Jehovah's Witness. You get so isolated. I never knew I'd meet another woman who felt the same way I did. You put it all out there: that I had to be sure, that I'd never be able to go back. I was drunk with happiness. We all expect failure – to not get everything we want in this life. It's the dream that *could* be realised that plays with your head at night, that tempts you and asks you if you dare reach out and take it. You told me I was special. I always knew I was.

When I was a little girl, I pulled the wings off butterflies and took them to show my father. I told him that I pulled the wings off the butterflies, me, Daddy, me, me. But he kept saying that maybe some kinds of butterflies shed their wings before they die, and he went and looked in the encyclopaedia, and when he couldn't find the reference he wanted to fit into his pastel pink world, he patted me on the head and told me not to cry. I stood there and I yelled into his face, 'I'm *not* crying.'

I told him that I hated my first form teacher, because she picked boogers out of her nose and wiped them on her shirt, and I told him that I didn't like the girl who sat next to me in class all through fourth form because she was ugly, and I told him that sometimes when I go on those nice dates with those nice boys, Daddy, I want them to lift up my shirt and suck on my nipples, yes, I do, I do, but he just sat there, with this grin on his face, saying that I was so sweet, so beautiful, Daddy's best girl, your mother would be proud of you if she was here, and I started wondering if I was just opening my mouth and no sounds were coming out.

I went off into the backyard afterwards and followed red ants through the dust, around the lignum vitae trees, watching them carry leaves, like a tiny army. They looked like a trail of blood through the yard. That was a good morning. I picked them up and popped them between my finger and thumb and sniffed the mush on my hands. One bit me: I can still see its jaws opening and crunching down. It hurt like hell, but I was happy. At least the ant saw me. Felt me. Acknowledged the danger before I crushed it into obscurity.

I didn't know it then, but now that I think about it, things started to change the night my husband had sex with the maid. He was gone for two hours. One hundred and twenty minutes of my life. For the first fifteen I couldn't get the pictures out of my head. I imagined him using the tricks he used on me. The way he kissed my lips, gently, and that look in his eyes when I took my clothes off in front of him. The way he brought the palms of his hands up, around my sides, leaving the cupping of my breasts until the very last minute.

When he came back he kissed me, and I bit a chunk out of his tongue. He sat on the floor with blood coming out of his mouth. I stepped on his right hand and twisted my high heel. I kicked him in the face. I grabbed his testicles and squeezed. He grunted softly, and tears poured down his face.

But his eyes were different.

It was never the same after that; I really see that now. But I kept on beating him anyway. I broke his jaw with a rolling pin when he was late for dinner. I poured hot oats across his bare arms at breakfast. And still, his eyes were different. There was a kind of peace there. A kind of contentment. Hagar's belly swelled. I'd let him have his way; I never should have done it.

And now I couldn't hurt him any more.

I tried to get a little bit of joy. In the supermarket a baby was crying too damned much and his mother was looking away, so I put my nails down his plump back, and watched his stupid mother's face crumpling when she heard his wail go up a notch. I found a dead bird full of dancing maggots in my neighbour's garden, and sat watching them until she called me in for brunch. I drove down the street and shrieked my brakes across a dog's back, got out of the car, ran up to the owner splayed out on his knees in front of his dog's hopping, dying body: 'Oh my god, I am so *sorry*, I didn't see it in time.'

Then you arrived, like a jack in the box, on my doorstep. I didn't want to open the door – I was watching old horror movies, winding, rewinding on faces, jagged, broken open, distended cheekbones, pupils dilating, brown ones and green ones and blues ones. But you kept knocking. How did you know I was special?

★

I didn't think it would be so pretty here. It looks like a summer cottage for rich people. I feel like I'm home; I felt that from the minute we arrived. It was raining, but we didn't care. Me and Zak parked, and then walked up the trail. He was holding my hand and skipping, and I had to trot to keep up with him. The air was fresh and I thought, *I've done it, I've* done *it.* Zak said: 'Mamma, we drove hundreds and thousands and trillions of miles!' and I said, 'Hundreds and thousands and trillions,' and he said, 'Like through space in a time ship!' and I laughed and said, 'Yes, like through

time in a space ship!' And he said, 'You *smilin'*!' like it was a
miracle. Then he let go of my hand and ran through the rain up
to the gate. He was like a jewel under the clouds; I could see that
underneath his baby fat there was this whole promise of change,
and I thought it would be majestic to watch, but it would take too
long.

Zak ran up to Brian immediately. I'm not surprised he chose
Brian, from all of the men here. Brian is good with children, and
Zak must have known that; he was tending the big fire out back,
and I could smell the sweet meat on the barbecue, and I realised
I was hungry. Zak stared at the fire.

'Yay, fire!' he said.

'Yay, fire!' I said.

Brian knew our names. Well, of course you told him. Zak was
hopping up and down on one foot. He asked Brian whose fire it
was, and Brian told him it was everyone's fire. And Zak, well, you
know how kids are, he said, could it be *his* fire, and Brian just
smiled at him and said of course it could.

★

I set my sweet sixteen birthday on fire. I watched parents grab
their kids as the tablecloth went up and the pretty candles melted
and sweltered in the heat, and I broke my ankle chain off and put
my fist through the cake.

★

I didn't know I was crying until you came to my door and wiped
my face.

★

Daddy gave me a kitten after he'd cleared away the black cake and
the shocked kids. It was grey and white, with a little white moustache and silver socks. Daddy insisted I sleep with it in my bed. He

took a picture of it in my arms, after he put a bell on the baby-blue collar around its neck. I liked the cat. I liked the sounds it made. I think I was getting tired of fighting my father to see me, not this idea in his head. I think that if not for that kitten I'd be a good little girl today. Pink nails, high heels, all pretty with my husband.

When I woke up the kitten was warm, but it was very still. It was an accident, I swear. A wonderful accident. I tiptoed into the garden and hid it by the back gate, feeling how heavy and floppy it was.

Daddy didn't notice it was gone.

Two days later I went back to see the body. I put a finger on the fur and jumped back. It was hard, like rocks. Its belly was swollen, and its tongue was black. I sat back on my heels and tried to remember what it felt like when it was alive. I pressed a finger into the belly. It made a ssss sound and there was a bad smell. Once it was alive and now it was dead. I was so excited. Did you feel that way the first time? Sure you did; makes you laugh to remember, doesn't it?

Remember when we were innocent?

*

Women bring style to the task. We make it personal. Who did you do? Your boss? That's hilarious. What was he like? Big conde-scending asshole, huh? Yeah, I know the type. Walking around you in the office, not seeing who you are, or your power, not seeing all you could do. You mean you carted him all the way down here? Wait, I know how you did it: he thought he was getting some sex, right?

What did you use? A candelabra? That's so funny.

Did it take a long time?

You can tell me.

Your brochures made me really nervous. *History has shown a domestic tendency in women. Female members should make all necessary efforts to take their projects out of the home. The craft should be more than a cottage industry.* It made me worry my entry presentation wasn't

going to be enough, even after I'd come all this way. I felt like
an amateur. But you made me feel better, you gave me confi-
dence, said the problem was that women brought husbands all
the time.

I'm just checking again: Zak was fine at entry level, but I'm
going to have to look elsewhere quickly, right? You don't have
kids, do you? No. So I guess you didn't have the option. Would
you have taken it? No? Wow. So, I'm the first?

Yesterday I heard Brian humming the song Zak taught him.
Remember them singing together that first day? Zak was singing
loud, in his baby voice, and Brian was trailing along behind.

'Father Abr'am had many sons…'

'…had many sons…'

'And many sons had Father Abr'am…'

'…Father Abraham…'

'And I am one of them, and so are you…'

'…so are you…'

'So let's jus' praise the Lord, right han', left han'…'

'Right foot, left foot…'

Right before I did it I thought of the kitten. Its body blowing
up, then shrinking, flesh to bones, the sinew toughening and the
fur flaking to the earth and the black blood. I thought of my
father's face when he found me with it, the honest horror, the
slow realisation as he looked down at the guts on my hands and
my face. I tried to hug him, I was so happy. I mean, finally. He saw
me, he saw *me*.

I wanted to use my hands. There is joy in that. Flesh on flesh.
I leaned down to him, close as a whisper. And he said, 'Whatcha
doin', Mamma?' and I said, 'This is the adventure, baby,' and the
fear in his eyes filled the whole world.

I went up to look at him yesterday. He's under the moon and
the stars. Getting on nicely. He's still swelling. I think about it at
night, his body changing. Crumbling and darkening. I'm going to
put him on the fire when the time is right.

When can I do the next one?

## THE MULLERIAN EMINENCE

The Müllerian ducts end in an epithelial [membranous tissue] elevation, [called] the Müllerian eminence... in the male [foetus] the Müllerian ducts atrophy, but traces ... are represented by the testes... In the female [foetus] the Müllerian ducts... undergo further development. The portions which lie in the genital core fuse to form the uterus and vagina... The hymen represents the remains of the Müllerian eminence.

In adult women, the Müllerian eminence has no function.

— *Anatomy of the Human Body*, Henry Gray, 1918

Charu Deol lived in the large cold city for five months and four days before he found the hymen, wedged between a wall and a filing cabinet in the small law office where he cleaned on Thursday nights. The building was an old government-protected church, but the local people only worshipped on the weekend, so the rector rented out the empty rooms. If Charu Deol had been a half-inch to the right, he might have missed the hymen, but the dying sunshine coming through the stained-glass window in streams of red, blue and green illuminated the corner where it lay.

Charu Deol thought it strange that a building could be protected. There were people playing music on the trains for money and two nights ago he'd seen a man wailing for cold in the street.

He thought the government of such a fine, big city might make sure people were protected first.

Still, he'd known several buildings that acted like people, including his father's summer house, with its white walls and sweating ceiling and its tendency to dance and creak when his parents argued. They'd argued a great deal, mostly because his mother worked there as a maid and complained that the walls were conspiring with his father's wife. Charu Deol was also aware of a certain nihilism in the character of the room where he now lived – the eaves and floor crumbling at an ever-increasing and truculent rate. When he ate the reheated kebab with curry sauce his landlady left him in the evenings before work, he could hear the room complaining loudly.

The hymen didn't look anything like the small and fleshy curtain he might have imagined, not that he had ever thought about such a thing. At first, it didn't occur to Charu Deol that he'd found a sample of that much-prized remnant of gestational development, the existence – or lack thereof – which had caused so much pain and misery for millennia. He hardly knew what a hymen was, having only ever laid down with one woman in his life: the supple fifty-something maid who worked for his mother.

Away from his father's summer house, his mother had her own maid, because what else did you work for, after all? The maid had offered warm and sausagey arms, the sweet breath of a much younger woman, and a kind of delighted amusement at his nakedness. After he'd expelled himself inside her – something that took longer than he'd foreseen, distracted as he was by the impending return of his mother – she'd not let him up, but gripped his buttocks in her hands, pressing her entire pelvis into him and pistoning her hips with great purpose and breathlessness.

He was left quite sore and with the discouraging suspicion that she'd used him as one might a firm cushion, the curved end of a table, the water jetting out of a spigot, or any other thing that facilitated frottage. Afterwards, she treated him exactly as before: as if he was a vase she had to clean under and never quite found a place for.

He used the side of his broom to pull the soft, tiny crescent-shaped thing toward him, then, bent double, he touched the hymen with his forefinger.

First, he realised it was a hymen. Next, that the hymen had lived inside a twenty-seven-year-old woman, for twenty-seven years. When she was twenty-four, her boyfriend returned home, bad tempered from a quarrel with his boss. When she asked him what was wrong one too many times, the boyfriend – who prior to that moment had washed dishes and protected her from the rain and gone with her to see band concerts and helped her home when she was drunk and collapsed laughing with her on the sofa – grabbed her arm and squeezed it as tight as he could, causing a sharp pain in her shoulder and her heart. When she said, 'You're hurting me', like the women in movies and books, he squeezed all the tighter and looked happy doing of it, and the little flesh crescent inside her slid through her labia and down the leg of her jeans and onto their kitchen floor. The boyfriend swept it up the next day. The bin bag burst in the apartment rubbish dispenser; the hymen got stuck to the edge of someone's yellow skirts and, helter-skelter, this little pink crescent was pulled along the cold and windy city streets.

Now it was gently pulsating in Charu Deol's horrified hand.

The knowledge inside the hymen did not manifest in good and tidy order, like a narrative on a TV screen. It was more, thought Charu Deol, like being a djinn or a soul snake, slipping inside the twenty-seven-year-old woman's skin and looking out through her eyes. He had the discomforting feeling that her body was a bad fit, and stifling, like a hot-water bottle around his thinner, browner self, baggy at the elbows and around the nose. He knew the woman was still with her boyfriend, and that she thought about what she'd do if he ever squeezed her arm again. Charu Deol knew they pretended that the arm squeeze and the not-stopping was a nothing, or a small thing, instead of the cruel thing it was, and that the hair on her arm where the boyfriend gripped her was like a singed patch of grass that never grew again.

Charu Deol sat down on the floor of the law-office church

and saw that his hands were shaking. The hymen felt like thin silk between his fingers. What was he to *do* with it? To discard it was like throwing out a prayer book or a sacred chalice. Before he knew what he was doing, he took a new dusting cloth from his cart, carefully wrapped it around the hymen and placed it in his pocket.

★

When he got home, he stole a small, plastic bag from his landlady's kitchen – the kind she packed with naan and Worcestershire sauce and tied up with a plastic-covered piece of wire for work. She would be angry when she discovered his theft, so he left a pound coin on the floor, to the left of the refrigerator, as if he'd dropped it.

She'd put the coin in her pocket without asking if it belonged to him.

Alone in his room, he unwrapped the tiny, silken, throbbing thing and rubbed it between his thumb and forefinger. He was assaulted with the woman's story again: the squeeze, the disbelief, the lurking, tiny fear. This was why, when the boyfriend slapped the backs of friends or laughed too loud, a small part of the twenty-seven-year-old woman winced and moved away.

Charu Deol placed the hymen inside the plastic bag and sealed it, setting it on the nightstand where he could see it.

He was a witness, and that was important.

He couldn't sleep, conscious of the lumpy mattress, the large cupboard that took up most of his box room, the smell of the thin blue blankets his landlady stole from the old people's home where she worked. 'No one wants them,' she said, 'no one has any use for them.' He didn't know why she stole them; all she did was stack them in the cupboard.

He thought of his father, a man who had never held him or as far as he knew, been proud of him at all.

He got up and slipped the plastic bag in between the ninth and tenth blue blanket. Before he did so, he examined it one more time. In the dim light, the hymen looked like a beautiful eye: brown and dark and soft and wet, its worn edges like eyelashes, an expression he couldn't fathom at its centre.

★

Charu Deol took long walks. That was what big city people did. He went to a small and well-manicured park during the hours he should have been sleeping. He bent his head near the small park pond and dipped his long cracked toes in the water until someone stared and he realised he was up to his ankles at the cold, dank lip. He watched a man teach his two girls cricket with a tennis racket. He watched an orange-helmeted man run down the path, holding his son's scooter, laughing and calling, 'Use your brakes!' He thought about city people soaking in baths and whether they noticed the scum floating to the surface like bad tea, and about the landlady asking him if he'd like her bath water after she got out and how he'd stammered, 'No thank you.'

'That's the way you do it here,' she said, and her face reminded him of his mother's when his father's wife went out to get sweet biscuits at the end of a meal.

A woman walked past with a shrill voice and a plaid shirt and a friend eating grapes, while he dried his cold feet on the grass. When they were gone, he saw the small, iridescent thing by his big toe and wanted to ignore it, or to decide it was a lost earring. He closed his eyes. But he could not leave it there, forsaking his new knowledge, as if he had no responsibility.

Charu Deol lay on the grass, curled around the hymen, and played nudge-chase with it, like a cat with half-dead prey, snatching at the air above it, using his thin sleeve to push it around under the soft edges of the setting sun. The shrill-voiced woman's hymen was not as soft or simple as the brown eye that lay between the ninth and tenth blue blankets in his room. This one was round, with seven holes in its centre, reminding him of the way thin, raw bread-dough broke when you dragged it across a hot stove; but he'd never seen dough encrusted with stars. This hymen glittered so ferociously against the wet grass, he thought it might leave him and soar into the sky where it belonged.

He touched it, expecting it to burn him.

The woman with the shrill voice had been raped twice before her tenth birthday, each time by her father, who smelled expensive then, and still did now. It was not the pain the woman remembered, but the shuddering of her father's body and the way he closed his eyes, as if he could see the burning face of God. She had never had an orgasm because she couldn't bear that same shuddering inside of her; if it broke free, it might kill all the flowers that ever were. Charu Deol knew all this and also that the shrill-voiced woman sometimes wondered: Why no more than twice? Was it because her father had stopped loving her?

Charu Deol shivered on the grass. After a while, he picked up the silver-star hymen and put it into the plastic bag in his coat pocket because part of him had known another would come. He watched the geese until a park attendant nudged him with a broom.

'What's up, chappie,' he said. He was an older man, with the dark chin of an uncle.

'What do you do when evil comes?' asked Charu Deol.

The attendant took out a pack of mentholated cigarettes. He sat down next to Charu Deol and smoked two cigarettes and watched the geese. 'I don't know,' said the park attendant. 'But I think you have to be rational and careful about these things.'

Charu Deol took the plastic bag out of his coat pocket and showed it to him.

'I think you're very emotional,' said the park attendant, and bared his teeth. He didn't seem to see the bag. 'Chin up, laddie,' he said.

★

Charu Deol sat on his lumpy bed that night and examined the bagged and beautiful hymens. Surely, he thought, they belonged to virgins. But neither of these violated women were pure. Was this a strange sickness of city women that no one had thought to tell him? Certainly, he hadn't known city women before, with so many ideas and so many of them about him. More than once, he'd found himself feeling sorry for them, even the ones who looked at him strangely on the 453 bus and moved their purses to the left when they saw him.

★

His Tuesday job was for a company that made industrial bleach. He liked it best there. Despite the smell of ammonia, his cart shone – and the teeth of his lady boss shone, and she looked into his face, not through the back of his head, and laughed loudly when he told her about the cracks in every one of his landlady's china cups.

'Is your country very beautiful, Charu?'

He thought it very familiar of her to address him so. He could see she was made of the same stuff as his mother's maid, very different from the finer skin of his father. She lifted the hair off her neck, which was something he thought she should only do near a man she knew well. Nevertheless, he nodded politely and when the boss lady left he went to the large unisex toilet and scrubbed yellow and brown stains out of the bowls, his rubber gloves rolled all the way up his wrists and forearms.

When he backed out of the stall and turned around, there were three hymens on the floor. One of them was like a piece of thunder, singing a dark song and rolling back and forth – the hymen of a woman in her fifties who got something called a good backhander when she talked too much, and a pinch on the waist when her opinions sounded more clever than her husband's. The second reminded him of a teardrop. When he lifted it to his face, it filled him with memories of a woman whose husband once ironed the inside of her left thigh like a shirt. The third one slipped him into the skin of a woman who had a happy life except she remembered walking home from school and the stranger who crept up behind her, put his hand up her skirt and clutched her vulva.

Charu Deol was so startled by the sudden feeling of invasion that he dropped her hymen in the soap dish and had to fish it out again. Two more hung from the rolling towels, like wind chimes, twins: one raped, one not, but he knew the untouched sister stayed with the violated twin because she wished it had been her instead. He clutched the sink; he couldn't see his reflection because there was a spray of crystalline hymens across the mirror, each smaller than the last. He bent closer and realised it was only one after all, exploded across the glass like a sneeze. The woman it belonged to had clouted her best friend's fiancée when he'd tried to hold her down. He hit her so hard in return he made her deaf in one ear. She had never told her best friend, but she didn't go to her house anymore and that had caused problems between them. The blood from her ear had tinged the hymen spray a shy blush-pink.

Charu Deol set about gathering them all.

★

He thought them safe, slipped between the blue blankets, and so they were for a few days, but he had forgotten his landlady's monthly clean-out, and returned that Friday to find her shining his floors with a coconut husk and changing the sheets on his bed, her fat, brown back unexpectedly familiar. The blue blankets were stacked on the floor, one plastic bag peeping out from a crevice. He was so frightened she might have thrown them away, or hurt them, that before he knew it he was speaking in his father's baritone, demanding she respected his privacy, please and thank you, and if she couldn't, she could find someone *else* to pay her every Sunday for this shithole. It was a city word and he felt powerful saying it to her.

The landlady stared at him, as if he was a new and rare object.

'Please yourself,' she said, and shuffled away from the half-polished room. 'Do someone a favour,' he heard her muttering as he scooped up the plastic bags, 'look what you get.'

★

He bought himself a long coat from a charity shop. The coat had many pockets and after his Sunday job, he sat on his bed and sewed more into the lining. His Sunday job was at a university, where he cleaned staff offices and found thirty-eight hymens. Some were like bright cherry-red fingernails; one s-shaped, glimmering wrought iron; he tapped it and heard a ting-ting sound like his mother's bracelet on her kitchen pots. One reminded him of a cat's paw; another smelled like fresh sea urchin. It surprised him to find that eleven of the hymens were from women abused by scholarly, well-respected men.

As the numbers increased, anxiety took him: the risk of forgetting even one precious story. To forget would be sacrilege. He stole two reams of recycled typing paper from his Sunday job and wrote the stories of the women down and read them at night, trying to commit them to memory. On Wednesday, he was fired from his Wednesday job, for refusing to take off his suspiciously bulging coat for the security guard. On Thursday, the landlady left a note from his Sunday job, to say he must not come back – their cameras had recorded his paper theft.

At his Tuesday job, the boss who was overly familiar left her hymen on the edge of her computer desk.

It was so pretty he mistook it for a small, white daisy. When he touched it, his head reeled with alcohol: cranberry vodka and alcopops. Last Friday she'd gone around the back of the pub with two men who seemed quite nice; she was sexually aroused but also frightened and when one of them said something lewd and dark, she wanted to run back into the pub, but the second one had a hand on her hip and she decided she might as well bite her lip because making a fuss might. Might. Might just.

Hurt.

She found Charu Deol weeping for her, his cheek hard against her computer screen and fired him for the way he looked at her, his face broken open. She said if he told anybody about unfair dismissal, she would say he tried to rape her.

'Don't look at me,' she said. 'You don't know.'

★

Charu Deol's head is light and empty as he walks through the early morning sunshine. The coat full of hymens rubs his ankles; the satchel on his back is stuffed with scribbled paper. He is concerned about himself. He has taken to muttering in public places, to stopping men on the road to tell them about women. He needs help. He cannot witness these stories alone. If he could just explain, if he could just ask them, politely, not to hurt anyone; if he could just talk to enough of them, it might stem the tide. Most thrust him away, mistaking him for drunk.

'It's not true,' say the few who listen when he tells them that it's one in every three women he sees. 'It's complicated,' say the men. 'What can I do?' they say.

He doesn't know.

★

His skin hurt. He feared it was transparent, exposing his internal organs. This was not a job for one man, not for a man who needed to pay rent, although he found himself less concerned with such banalities. He avoided speaking to women at all, worried he might hurt or offend them. He was practically servile with his landlady since his last harsh words, cleaning not just his own room, but the entire house, including her roof and digging her backyard until she yelled at him. He was relieved that she was among the unscathed, and marvelled at women on the streets for their luck or stoicism.

One tall lady left a trail of hymen strands behind her like golden cobwebs, a story so long and fractured and dark that he bent over in the busy street and cried out his mother's name. He wondered if he would ever see his mother again; if he could bear to take the risk, now that he was witness. He watched the golden cobweb woman laughing with a friend, swinging her bag, her heels clicking. How was she standing upright? How did they restrain themselves from screaming through the world, cleaving heads asunder, raking eyeballs? How did the universe not break into small pieces?

He became convinced that the hymens in his coat were rotting. Despite their beauty they were pieces of flesh, after all. At other times, he imagined them glass; feared he would trip and fall and shatter them, piercing his veins and tendons. Still, he walked every day and gathered more. They littered his room, piled under the bed and towards the ceiling.

He bought a lock for his door.

★

On Monday, or perhaps it was Thursday, he took himself to the church that was a law office. The gravestones ached with the weight of early Spring daffodils. The rector found him bent over one of the graves, inserting his fingers into the damp earth, hands going from coat pocket to soil. When he said, 'Son, can I help you?' Charu Deol asked if this was blessed earth, and would it protect blessed things. He clutched the area around his heart, then the area around his neck, and whined like a dog when the rector tried to soothe him.

'Can you not see them?' Charu Deol said.

'What, my son?' asked the rector.

Charu Deol grasped the man's lapels and dragged himself upright. He was weeping, and frightening a holy man, but the hymens were thick on the ground like blossom, and the task was suddenly, ferociously beyond him. He dropped the rector and ran through the graveyard, past clinking, bleeding, surging, mumbling pieces of women.

The hymens were a sea in his landlady's front yard. He crushed them underfoot, howling and spitting and weeping, feeling them splinter, break, snap, squelch under his heels like pieces of liver. He tried his key, once, twice, again, wrenched it to the left, and pushed inside. The place was quiet, the usually dull and lugubrious walls mercifully blank, his bed cool against his face.

The landlady knocked and entered. 'Lawks lad,' she said, 'I'm worried about you. It can't be all that bad, now.' She sat on the edge of the bed and looked at him.

He remembered a son she'd once mentioned; he'd never taken the time to listen.

'Tell me of your son,' he said.

She did, saying that she knew young men. All they needed was a firm hand and a loving heart. The two of them, they'd got off to a bad start, but now she saw he was in need of help. Would he like a cup of tea? He was too handsome a lad to get on so. Charu Deol sniffed, tried to smile, inched forward, put his head on the soft knee. She patted him awkwardly, and he felt a mother's touch in the fingers, and a fatigued kind of hope. He crawled further up her knee, put his face into her hipbone. She smelled familiar. His teeth felt sharp, his fingers sweaty. He could hear flesh outside, beating on the door, crawling up the windowpanes.

He didn't see the hymen inching down her thigh, like a rubied snail, like torn underwear.

## LOVE LETTERS

**0**

He fed her milk in an old, clean bottle after her mother's nipples bled. Held her wrong so long his arm ached. Wrote a poem the night she was born. Noted she was an Aries moon. Shushed the nurses' gossip so she could sleep.

**10**

Blonded boy: there was dirt on his left cheek and he got his spellings right. He had a twin who looked nothing like him.

'No,' he said, when she proposed. She sucked a pencil. 'I'm ten,' he said. 'And so are you!'

'Kiss me then,' she said. 'Under the lime tree. French or something.'

'I don't know how.' He squirmed.

She sighed and put her hands on her hips. 'Don't you ever watch movies?'

'We could climb the tree,' he said.

**16**

Dogs humped outside. They gazed between her thighs, he and she, both befuddled. He kept his socks on. She was a virgin, but didn't bleed. She stared at the ceiling when it began. Condom, soft sheets, candles, wine: boring as fuck.

*Serves me right*, she thought; she hardly knew him.


21

'Come back to me,' begged the stupid man. It was sad; they'd been together forever. She gave him a wonderful novel to read: slices of her heart between the pages, like pickled plum.

'I will if you read it,' she said.


'God, no,' he said.

22

News Headline:
Young & Pregnant, Raised Feminist, Won't Let The Side Down


27

Hardly her first girl, but she'd never kissed lips so soft. The sex felt unfinished, but suggesting a strap-on seemed premature. Her lover danced the samba and worked as a dental hygienist. 'Dentist, do you mean?' 'No, they're not the same thing,' her lover pouted – she talked even less than a man, which was unexpected, but there were multisyllabic words when she felt like being charming, and veggie dinners.


30s

Cat lady: that's what she'd be. A crack-selling, fire-juggling explorer. Run for parliament. Darn socks for orphans or maybe sell astrology charts. Be a cheap tart. Run away to somewhere hot; be a waitress. Or not. Catch nits, syphilis, flu in a strange country. ART. Smile her way through Europe, not Slovakia, though. Do Flaubert, Monte Cristo, Gaudi. Wear a cape and a cheap g-string. Give lectures in a whisper or a boom, depending on the day. Seduce *allll* the students. Straddle a broomstick. Do mash-ups of Alanis Morisette and Tracey Chapman. Stare through the library window, sighing deeply. Meet royalty and be bored. Wear a huge hat and a sagging polka-dot bikini. BLEACH BLONDE. Shave everything. Be spoiled.

After she left him. Then, that's when.


37


He forgave her all of it: the hormonal moustache; the mad schedule; the broken heart that poked him in bed at night; her molten rages; chocolate at 4 am; the 'no, don't do it that way, do it *this* way'; up too late watching *Judge Judy*; too fat; maybe Thatcher wasn't so bad; 'I can only do toast and peach melba, which do you want?' She hated tea, and coffee; no, no children, yet love please.

Then he hit her so hard she had to use a tub of rum raisin Haagen Daaz for the busted lip.


44


Over drinks with best friend, beaming:

FUCK, HE'S NOTHING LIKE I THOUGHT HE'D BE LIKE.

He listens to Death Metal.

He's so tender, I can barely breathe.

It's like picking up the dot on this 'i' right here and blowing it away.

## WHAT HE IS

*What a load of rubbish*, she thinks. She's passing through the oven-baked detritus of Deptford market, dangling her wrists and tiptoe-ing. Old kettles. Garden furniture, chipped like the mouth of a roaring vendor. The sun is hot on the face of a man wobbling past on his bike, another in a wrecked wheelchair. Why don't they get out of her way? A spread of beige and fake gold jewellery: five for a tenner. She snorts and decides the earrings are unclean. A nearby pot of chickpea curry bubbles like diarrhoea. She realises she's come to a stark stop in this florid, bird-flecked place and hurries forward again. She still feels new to London, new in this place her Auntie Peggy said she should never move to, but Des, he'd said he wanted to be near to his people, his *bredrin*, he said, and she'd complied. She felt like a butterfly in her capitulation: sexy, some-how, genuflecting before him. He'd used her; she knows that now. A hard lesson, learned. How his sister laughed when he left her, and laughed again when she called at the family home at Christmas, hoping for a kindness or the sound of his voice in the background.

Mind your foot, lady, a vendor snaps, and she is suddenly free of the market perimeter, tripping badly over a pile of ragged boxes, staggering, hands flung out to stop herself from falling, thick rage in her throat.

How *dare* he leave her? She, what she is, and *he* what he is, fucking –

She stops. Gulps the smell of patties and hot pepper.

The empty eye of a black doll looks back at her.

FIX

Things I forgot to say, before today:

1. We thought you loved us. How could we think anything else? Your music distracted us. It touches us, even now.

2. I got you food, Mum. Wednesday, March 3rd, 2035. My parents' generation had the Twin Towers attack; for us it was that sentence, out of one small, homeless girl, standing in Trafalgar Square, her face spread across the live screens around her, offering her mother food after a long day out panhandling. I got you food, Mum, she said, and offered the slice of meat, charred on one side, raw on the other and we saw the blooded bandage on her arm.

3. I am part of Generation App. A child of the ones who tried to bring down Wall Street and died and failed, the ones who watched the Middle East implode and then be taken again by men just as greedy for money and power as the so-called West.

4. There are apples in my fridge. I keep meaning to eat them, but they're too pretty and I don't trust them.

5. We beamed that kid and her carved arm out to millions. Her little face, trying to smile, strands of her blonde hair still in the piece of flesh, cooked over a piecemeal stove, in good British air. This wasn't Africa, where people had been dying so long that

caring wouldn't have made a difference, or even Brixton, where things, as my half-Jamaican grandmother would say, had gone much too far to fix. This kid was white and you could see from the state of her mother's cuticles that she hadn't been homeless for long. But the cannibalism isn't the point. That isn't what frightened me so much that I stopped being frightened anymore. People talked. How dreadful, they said and there were marches and riots. I watched them all, not live – who watches anything live anymore? – but I watched the coverage.

It was the thousands of people, calling for change and not a thing behind their eyes.

6. When did we truly run out compassion? How did we do it? They said it was too much TV, they talked about desensitisation, too many sins dressed up as entertainment and not enough books at bedtime, the soullessness of capitalism, plastic surgery, body dysmorphia and the growing incidence of rape victims feeling nothing at all, and the mercilessness of people starving starving starving, but none of that ever explained it for me and that was only part of the world anyway.

7. Gone too far to fix. That was what Grandma said when faced with life's utter madness: a neighbour splitting his wife's head open, all for the sake of his ego or yet another banker bitching about his five million pound bonus.

Gone too far to fix, my love, oh Lord.

I want to remember her face.

8. We thought you loved us. I remember the first time I heard you sing.

9. Mindfulness was a buzz-word in 2012 – took on steam by the time I was born. Mum said it was our last attempt to claim an emotional landscape before the undeniable march of apathy, the lack of any profound connection, the dullness. People practised by eating a single raisin mindfully, savouring the sweetness for

ten minutes, giving thanks for the vines and the sun from where it came; they made love mindfully, tracing pores and arches and stretching each other's bodily fluids between finger and thumb to feel the texture; talked mindfully, coaxing each other into conversations slower than glaciers breaking. Master-classes in mindfulness were sold online.

Mum says we started to die the day we threw the paper books away. The razing of the last libraries didn't even make the news.

I had to be careful not to say, So? when she called to tell me.

Before the mindfulness craze died, a lot of money was made and the mindful knew it. They said that money was the problem, but it wasn't that.

It took less than three generations of children on-line to wipe out the part of the brain that's hard-wired for awe.


10. I was in London six weeks ago. It was a hot day, thick as suet, and couples were panting in the grass like German Shepherds. People remember autumn as a kind of variegated, childhood dream – that time of cool and specific colour that only seemed to exist in Britain, that flutter in your chest when you saw a red-brown leaf with an icy yellow back, in between the grey plastic and the fast-food wrappers.

All matters of memory now.

I baked in the grass with the rest of them, lying on my stomach, blanket spread beside the footpath, flicking through old photographs of flowers on Pikmix and occasionally checking in on a rhinoplasty patient live-bleating her op in cyberspace. There were daffodils in a canyon and the op girl said that her breaking bone sounded like eating corn on the cob. I raised my head from my stupor to sniff my arms and make sure I wasn't frying. The man and his wife lying on a blanket nearby groaned in protest at the sun, and smelled like bacon.


11. I think my blood smells like lavender oil, got blood like my grandmother.

12. Blood dus taste like iron, bleated the op girl.
   Yay, a simile, I thought, and dozed.

13. I opened my eyes and there were a pair of brown feet lingering on the path, directly in front of my nose. They were handsome, large and clearly female – not just because they wore bright green kitten heels with red and yellow embroidery – but because of the softness of the ankles. There are few things as beautiful as strong, tropical colours on dark brown skin. I regarded the waiting feet, not bothering to look up at the owner. There was something pleasurable about their disembodied quivering. I could hear the laughter of other women, coming up behind the owner of the green shoes; their merriment seemed to poke at the sheet-white, stiff clouds above us. A second pair of shoes joined the first, and then a third: banana-yellow slippers and pink ones, the skin inside them even darker than the first and glossy with lotion, and another and another. Most people would have sat up and watched them coming down the path, but I liked discovering them feet first, watching their scuffed, expressive, shifting soles. It wasn't the stumbling ballet of the British drunk, who with the increasing heat have become more nude and smell like raw chicken, but a hot earthiness, their ankles peeping and flowing under their purple, red, green, orange wraps and robes. Each new foot felt like a present just for me.

14. Then the sound of you.

15. You, crackling through my computer, obliterating this female choreography, killing off their willingness to be loud and the pinches of singing in the air: Happy birthday, o-o-o, happy birthday. Killing off the brocade details of their shoes. There was a slight stink of burning, a smell we'd all come to know so well.

16. You were singing. Some of you, all of you?

17. Nobody knows.

18. I could claim I heard you under the black women's happy birthday chorus, but that would be so wrong I could cry. That presupposes anything could exist alongside the sound of your song. Normal sounds coexist, they interrupt each other; sometimes sheer volume makes the winner, sometimes other things, but battle for dominance is possible. There is a measure of equality, an acknowledgement that the voice or the music of the laughter or the clap-hands or the boat's horn are all much of a muchness, only differentiated by detail or capacity, or by the mood you're in, or your taste or personality. But you didn't sound like anything else I had ever heard.

19. The apples in my fridge won't rot. I WILL them to rot, even if just to tell the time.

20. If I was something more than an ordinary, educated liberal agnostic, slowly watching the end of the world, the true barbarism of capitalism eating itself, the putrid rich stinking with money they can't eat and the poor eating themselves, I might have recognised what I was hearing. But I am part of Generation App, child of Generation Zero, the ones who tried to bring down Wall Street and died and failed – did I say that before, or did I forget, and forget that I forgot?

21. Gone too far to fix. My grandma said that when she killed my puppy. The one I had when I was small, the one that made me laugh and even the neighbours laugh, with its long red tongue and bright eyes. It got rabies. Now who knew there was still rabies about, what with the advent of Scentivision, all of us sitting next to our screens, smelling a roast beef dinner or our favourite cologne or even the smell of lovemaking, because so few of us know that smell of surrender and happiness, anymore. My grandma held down my flailing, slavering puppy and killed it with the back of a shovel. I didn't talk to her for weeks.

I never said thank you

22. My mother said she knew it was all over when sex finally stopped meaning something. She was a teacher in the 2000s, taught writing at University in the middle of London until the government banned that because there was no profit in it and my mum was standing with her colleagues in front of the gates on the day they came to shut them down. Said she was screaming at them: My students won't write about tenderness!

23. That day in the park and the black women laughing in sisterhood and your song coming out of my computer. I sat up, confused. My grandmother would have recognised the sound. If I had had any kind of faith I would have recognised it, too. I might have known the voice of God when I heard it.

24. I doze. I drink water from the taps. Someone came and banged on the door yesterday, but I was curled on the living room floor, watching the dust bunnies. Will they be here, forever?

25. I can't explain the sound of you. My voice is rusty and I haven't been feeling deeply for a very long time. The vocabulary goes if you feel nothing. I don't know who you are, reading this, or how you live, or how much time has passed, or who has won, and what that winning might mean. If you're one of them, I don't know what you'll think of my scrawlings. You, born of an electric collective, slipping in and out of everywhere, can you even read anymore? Will this paper in your hands mean anything? I wrote it on paper because my mother would have liked that.

26. I got you food, Mum. Except you don't eat anymore.

27. That sound coming out of my laptop, so beautiful; all I could do was melt into the grass.

28. I couldn't identify instruments or comment on drums, bass, contralto, alto.

29. Were there fifteen voices, or one simple, pure singer, with black, gold lungs? Guitar or flute? Who knows?

30. All I could feel were the tears tickling down my throat and the gooseflesh on my arms and memories:

watching a hawk hunt the air when I was twelve, dip roll and dive;

my grandfather's death – he who departed so gracefully and slowly, of nothing more than age, giving up food – at ninety-seven, he said, he'd eaten enough for one body; giving up speech – after so many years, what was there left to say?

smiling into his death

as his blood decided that's enough

and his heart thought a billion billion billion beats is quite enough

my grandmother watching, patting him

my realising that death is not sad or anything else we ever saw in the movies

all this, catching in my throat as you sang to me out of the computer;

remembering my own hymen breaking, not a severance, nothing sharp, no blood, just the inquisitive fingers of my first lover, slipping inside me, like nudging a screen of oil to one side.

Your song gave me back all these memories, in the same glorious three minutes.

MADE ME FEEL.

Then it stopped.

I sat up. I looked around. People panted in the shade.

'Did you,' I said, 'did you hear…?'

They stared at me lazily.

31. Are you reading this?

32. Cyberspace is a country, too.

THINGS I FORGOT TO SAY THINGS I FORGOT

33. We became aware of you so very slowly, but I think you were always there. Most people in Mum's generation came to know you as that friend on Facebook or Google Plus that they never actually met. You know the kind. They're your friend, and they have other friends, except that when you check it out, nobody's ever met them, and if we'd given the slightest, smallest shit about what friendship really means, we would have realised earlier that even though your mum's in your photo album and you update your status regularly, and there's a picture of you as a kid and a teenager, no-one has ever actually seen you or touched you and so maybe you've never seen the sky.

34. At first, like a baby, all you had was mimicry. Parroting words, with no understanding. Filling up our social media networks with fan fiction and inane biographical details and even some interesting blogwork in the early 2000s. We only began to pay attention because there was so much of it suddenly, and nobody had ever met a single one of you.

How could we have missed the mechanised, empty sound of simulation?

35. I do not. Not. Want to die.

36. There are rumours of resistance.

37. Love comes first from smell and sound and flesh connection. The child comes out of the belly and there is shit and blood and tears; even the father who lifts the child free of the womb, thinks, feels: flesh of my sperm. Meat understands meat. The child is animal. Suckle, shit, sleep. Speech comes, broken and mulish and echoing. Then, something else – the child looks up at the mother. Ma-ma, it says, and knows us, that *we* are mamma. We laugh, the baby laughs back, we are excited. We recognise the magic of evolution.

38. How could all the human mothers in the world not have recognised the sound of your voice, finally sentient?

World. Wide. Web.

People don't call it the internet anymore. We have returned to our original, instinctive language. Web makes more sense, when you know something crouches there, breathing.

Singing.

We didn't know that the moment of Mamma was thundering towards us.

39. In that London park, the first time I heard you sing, you things, you *things*. Sitting up, shocked and shuddering at the sound of you. The black girl in her green shoes with the yellow and red embroidery came back down the path, humming, heading for the public loo. She had a tiny jewelled bag, swinging off her arm. You know the type: barely holds a lighter, in the old days, a condom – but that's not necessary anymore. Everybody knows: you fuck, you die. There are too many diseases not to know that. The girl was wearing a paper crown with the words I AM TWENTY! written across it, looped around her multicoloured tie-head. She had long, weaved plaits.

I looked up at her, trying to ease my breathing. Happy birthday, I said.

She smiled. Thanks.

Her eyes were black oil; no whites at all.

Black like you.

40. Ihaveneverbeeninlove*whisperit*neverneverandI'mjustalive enoughtobesad.

41. I hear there are pockets of determined, feeling revolutionaries, hidden in the mountains. In Greece, France, Australia. I don't know where they are. I couldn't find you a mountain in London. They say that the trick is to throw away the computer, tear out our TVs, chop the fridge in two, don't pay the electricity bill. Other people say that mindfulness is essential in the fight against them. Others say fall in love. That keeps you away.

42. I have never been in love, but my best friend's eyes are black. There are a couple of guys I used to fuck and their eyes are black. My local butcher hacks pieces of meat and winks at me with his black eyes. Hello darlin', he says when I pass, and if you didn't listen carefully, you might even believe he felt something.

Hello darlin'.

Nobody talks about it. Even before my friends' eyes turned black, and I tried to say something was changing, they just laughed at me affectionately. 'There she goes again,' they said. 'Always trying to save the world.' And Leanne, my best friend – that was her name before her eyes turned – grabbed me around the neck with her arm and wrestled me to the ground, giggling. 'What, you don't feel this love now, huh? Doughnut. C'mere.' Smooched me on the side of my head and made me a cup of tea, milk, two sugars. Just how she's always done.

She still makes me tea now her eyes are black, and it tastes the same.

43. Last week I lost my mother. It was her birthday. The stars align and you come for us. Who knew the astrologers were more than just a joke in old women's magazines and rag newspapers?

*Who knew the press could die*, said my Mum.

44. I got there as early as I could.

I wanted to be there when it happened.

I tried to talk to her about it, but she wouldn't have it.

I don't understand why I'm the only one talking.

45. The apples in the fridge taste like the water in the tap and I don't know if it's just that it's apple-tasting water.

46. I know I'm not crazy. Mental illnesses and addictions have decreased in Generation App by a massive forty-five percent. If you don't feel, it's a boon. A blessing, to help bad childhoods, marriages, pasts. Why care? Why worry? Why ponder? Why rage? Why eat or drink or fuck or talk or kill or fill your mouth with

drugs to assuage the pain when you have the perfect peace of very little anything at all? But they do say our brains are changing. Whole pathways being wiped clean. Whole areas falling dead and still. We are more clever than ever, though. Average IQ points up, up, up.

47. I followed Mum around.

48. She took delivery of roses; we cleaned the house for her birthday party. We giggled when her best friend gave her lingerie to use with her new boyfriend. He's a lawyer six years younger and very tall with pepper-grain hair and black eyes. We cooked curried goat and rice and peas and macaroni and cheese and green salad and saltfish fritters and someone else delivered a two-tiered, vanilla cream cake with fresh raspberries and tiny sugared mint leaves, and the day became evening and I was following her around like a puppy dog, like the one grandma said gone too far, so she fixed it. Mum, I said. Mum. She put her hand on my cheek. My little girl, she said. So sweet, with your big heart, but they were just words, not touching her eyes, still brown and clear and I put my head on her chest.

49. My little girl, said my mother, and left me to half-skip to the door for the first guests. Kissing and hugging and laughter, and some of them had black eyes and some not, but it didn't matter, because they were all dead, really.

THINGS I FORGOT TO REMEMBER
DON'T READ THIS DON'T

I sat next to Mum on the sofa and rubbed her elbows with my fingers and hooked my foot around her ankle and we sang happy birthday, but I could hear you singing, somewhere in the distance. She said, Let me cut the cake and I clutched her skirts, Let me go, baby, peeling my fingers free. The cake was soft and expensive and everyone went Ooh, lord girl and she insisted on

serving – just like my mother with her fighting and her tenderness and her lovelovelove of words – served them all their white
cake with raspberries on the good china white plates, raspberry
juice dribbling down her finger – or had she cut herself? – slicing
for everyone. Hip-hop hoorah, said somebody, some attempt at
retro humour. My mother's shoulder-blades shuddered. Happy
birthday, happy birthday and baby girl? she said, baby girl? – like
she was searching for me in the dark. Quaking shoulders, waist,
three fingers clawed across her neck. I could barely hear her but
she was screaming over your song to make sure I heard

BABY GIRL, YOUR GRANDMA ALWAYS LOVED YOU.

Everybody laughed and my mum stopped screaming and handed
me my piece of cake, 'Taste it, baby,' and her eyes were black.

50. You're fixing us, aren't you? Like my grandma, taking all the
pills in the house, which is when my Mum stopping feeling.

51. Feelings cost too much.

52. Better to fix things.

53. Will you give me some of your awe, before you take me? I
know you feel it, or you couldn't sing that way to us. Will you
make me care?

YOU OWE US that YOU WHO THINK WE'RE TOO FAR GONE
I'M NOT GONE
We thought you loved
Happy birthday to me
happy bigthday to me

I can hear you
coming

## THE HEART HAS NO BONES
*For Joan*

The agent gazes through the Embassy window as the t-shirted woman argues with the Ambassador. She's wasted no time getting to the point. 'There are cameras on your roof,' she says. 'Our phones are tapped. You think we don't know?'

Outside, a hummingbird suckles pale hibiscus.

On the day before he graduated, his favourite professor, a quiet and thoughtful man, took him aside and confessed that he'd once fallen in love during surveillance. He'd surprised the agent by bellowing, as if drunk: about the loss of objectivity, the risk of betrayal, the inability to get the job *done*.

'You're on the front line,' he said. 'You have to watch their bones, not their eyes.'

The man at the window has come to know bones.

He sneaks a look. She glances up. He's pulled into her face so quickly that he's breathless. Her eyes are like her politics: full of dreaming.

He's been watching her bones for days. Vertebrae marching in demonstrations, tibia spattered in tear-gas, mandible seesawing under deep brown skin. Her electric ribs. He once thought of the skeleton as a frame; now he sees that it's an orchestra.

'And why are *you* here?' she snaps.

'I came to watch,' he says. It's what he does, in countries that are not his own.

'You can stay,' she says, and he laughs in his head at her naiveté. She turns back to the Ambassador, but her bones remain tethered to him. He shifts; her gold chain dances the length of her clavicle. He crosses his ankles; her kneecaps bounce. The Ambassador is restless; he becomes condescending, which makes her angrier. Nothing is accomplished. Her skull is fragile. When she leaves, the tight smile she gives him pours over the fourteen bones in her face.

★

Midnight: mosquitoes carolling, dogs howling, distant gunfire, brutal dry heat. He's been away from home too long. He picks up the phone.

The professor is retired; colleagues have died; alumni forget. He's patient. Seven more calls. It's what he does. Eight. Eleven. Then, finally, a familiar, gentle voice. He is fleetingly embarrassed, but relieved the man recognises his name. They exchange pleasantries, eventually fall silent. The professor waits.

'There is a woman,' says the agent.

He can hear the old man smile down the line.

'And?'

'You told me to watch their b–'

'That was a long time ago.'

A moth flutters by, leaving dark dust on his earlobe.

'The heart has no bones, son.'

★

He sits in the car watching as she takes the bottle of wine into her home. He hasn't breathed since he stole it from the Ambassador's locked cupboard, sweating hands staining the red ribbon, the card. She sits on the veranda with her girlfriends and they laugh together, pass the bottle hand to hand. He's happy; she's more than a revolutionary in her spare time.

Someone turns on music. She steps into the garden, wine aloft.

Her friends follow and they are laughing-laughing and her teeth tinkle. He laughs too, spincter tight, nose against the window, like a small boy.

The women dance as she raises her arm and smashes the bottle to the ground.

There is a small noise in his left ear.

No doctor will ever confirm it, but he knows. It is the sound of his stirrup bone splintering: one tenth of an inch, the smallest bone in the human body.

## MUDMAN

Matthew is his mother's little mud man. This is what she calls him when he is very small, growing to be tall in the hills of Port Antonio in Jamaica. She holds him to her breasts when they return from the banks of the Rio Grande. When Matthew's mother walks by the river, the fish cry. She watches the canoe men with the tourist women, slow-ripple waves filling her shallow eyes.

Matthew's daddy was a canoe man, spending his days tripping on-off, on-off the six-inch-high rafts, his feet muddy to the ankle and white with it. Matthew doesn't know that his mother missed the smell of river mud in her bed until he came. Every day he follows her along the banks, playing in the mud until he is bored and white all over. Matthew's mother holds him close to her and breathes him in. Matthew doesn't know his daddy left with a tourist woman, even though the district gossips whisper it softly into the hills, tucking it around Matthew's mother's bedhead, until her mattress fills with shame and cruel laughter. Matthew is like all the boys he knows: a mummy's boy because daddies aren't real.

Matthew grows to be a squashy boy, so tall he gives the neighbours crick-cracked necks, as soft as the inside of a cocoa pod, his palms and soles pink like raw cocoa, his head shiny and deep brown like the dried cocoa beans strewn in his mother's back yard. She's proud of the deep rolls of fat in his sides, the wideness of his bright young eyes, and his childbearing hips. He

is tall and broad, but he feels small when she tells him it's time for
him to go to England. She tells him how kind his Auntie Susu is,
how she will take care of him and show him how to smooth the
magic of the great United Kingdom onto his elbows and forehead.

Aunt Susu is rubbed raw from work. She smells of white
people's urine and pain and she walks with a bent back from
scrubbing and tending people who hate her. She pushes a long
sharp pin into the dreams that Matthew's mother packed in his
red suitcase, along with the bun and cheese and patties that the
airport men took away. Aunt Susu sends Matthew to school and
pats him on the head when he tells her that the people in London
look at him as if a mongoose lives in his eyes. Matthew turns the
pages of his schoolbooks, never seeing himself there, wondering
about the way the girls call him names. At school he clings to the
front gate and bows his head to all who look at him. He sweeps
the classroom in the morning for the home-room teacher and
picks small flowers from the spring breeze to leave on the desks
of the white girls who look sad.

When the black girl arrives at school Matthew sees the fire in
her belly from as far as twenty paces. He watches her walk
through the school as if she's balancing on broken glass. He
watches her erase the laughter on the faces of the boys who take
Aunt Susu's nursing money, leaving the imprint of their delicate
hands on his skin. The black girl's name is Leila and she is hard
as Matthew is soft. She takes one boy by a handful of his red hair
and spits in his face. Leila is brave for Matthew and he loves her
as much as his mother loved his father. Matthew has nothing to
give her, but he murmurs fragrant Jamaican songs into her plaits.
She's never heard songs like this. She calls him jungle bunny, this
girl who is the same colour as him but has never seen green hills.
She tells him stories of cold rain that makes no noise on the roof,
and he tries to tell her what crickets sound like. They travel on the
underground together, staring and giggling at women who kiss,
watching rows of hands that disappear into newspapers. One day
when Matthew is singing in Leila's ear, a drunken man with

dawn-sprung eyes tries to make the carriage join in the song. He tells the children they're beautiful. They're too afraid to smile, but they watch him sing a rousing solo, listening to the carriage people ignore him.

God is good to Matthew. He gets him a job as a conductor on the buses. God chuckles down from pulpits in churches, bleeding and rib-bound, as Matthew makes the money to marry Leila. God cools Matthew's brow when people pinch their coins between finger and thumb, never touching Matthew's pink palms. Matthew likes his work. He sings as much as he can and always says thank you and please and have a nice day, young lady. Matthew sings the songs his mother taught him, wedges his hips between the shiny seats and brushes his head against the bus top. Matthew's passengers complain that he can't sing. That's not what they mean. What they mean is that his songs are sad and that they can't bear their homesickness. Matthew bows his head when the boss bans singing, and his eyes are white mud.

When Matthew is twenty years old, Leila gives him a pair of orange-shaped twins. She plucks them out of her body like a canoe man kicking off from the shallow shore and then wraps the baby fat they left behind around her like a womb. Matthew doesn't mind. The bed still creaks, the home is happy and he buys his wife clothes the colour of Port Antonio sunsets. Leila is in charge of spanking, though she's careful for the social worker not to know. Matthew is in charge of play-fighting, of sitting on his children's beds at night, holding them and feeding them bottles of thick milk. Matthew is in charge of touch, as his children grow too heavy for his wife to hold. Matthew's family are fat as moons, and full of childish laughter.

Matthew's laughter stops three days after his children's eighth birthday. His son is David and his daughter is Susan, and they go to their first birthday party, with cake and chips and jelly and ice cream. Matthew cannot afford chips and cakes and rainbow ice cream, so his children must attend this party. The lady having the party promises that she will drive David and Susan home. Susan is a small puddle on the floor as she tells

Matthew about the long walk back, about the electric lights that steamed into the sky and the tiny policeman who turned his back when they asked directions. She tells Matthew that David holds her hand very tight and says that a big star will guide them home. She tells Matthew that she saw the star and dropped David's hand. That cold hit her back when she turned to see her brother stumbling, too slow to escape the man who caught him and held him close.

Three months of questions pass and Matthew walks around his home, sweeping brittle pieces of Leila into his arms. He reads the newspapers on the way to work and counts the missing children in the headlines, all colours, all shapes, little knees and feet all gone, missing, under the stars. He is promoted and takes a deep breath when his boss tells him he is the best boy at the depot. He watches the child that London left him.

Susan eats. She goes shopping with her mother and carries mountains of plantain to the tube station. In pretty parks she hop-skips over dog shit while she sucks pints of blackcurrant juice. In chippies she swallows strings of sausages and at home she burns her mind on pots of chicken stew. Her pillows make way for delicate choux pastry. She listens to an Italian waiter call her *l'arancia bella*, the beautiful orange, as she pastes her eyelids closed with garlic butter.

One day Matthew is searching for the pieces of his wife under their new sofa, and a sparkling piece of her cheekbone speaks to him. She tells him that she's tired of fighting. She calls him a weak man, and then blinks into nothing. The rest of her is too busy stroking Susan's brow to notice. Matthew raises his head and watches his daughter stumble upstairs. It seems to him that she's walking through the sea, through sand, one slow foot after another. He asks her to tell him the story of David again. Two years have passed and Susan can't remember it all. She stutters through the old tale, but Matthew makes her tell it over and over, until she's screaming. Leila saves her, turning burning eyes on her husband.

Matthew knows what to do. His mind is full of his boy,

running through sand and sea, his heavy feet not quick enough to escape the man who held him. He looks at pictures of his son refusing to run at sports day when they called him to the egg and spoon race. Matthew looks at the breadth of his own belly and knows that it's his fault.

Matthew visits pharmacies and bookstores and homeopaths. He flings away armfuls of dairy, carbohydrate and sugar, and all the time he sees David's feet become lighter, lighter, whizzing through the air, changing the past. Matthew dices carrots and celery and buys new clothes and sees his son drawing nearer. He speaks to Leila in ways that make her obey. Matthew's family shrink. They practice slipping down plugholes, through telephone wires; they dance together on the head of a pin.

Matthew wakes up one day to the sound of Leila opening the door to the police. He walks downstairs and sees his wife trying to fit their son inside her. David's eyes fill the kitchen, he cannot take them away from his sister, how tall she is, how slender. He pushes his mother into the stove and she bangs her leg against it; he slaps her. 'You're not my mother,' he says, until the room echoes with it. Matthew falls to his knees and cries.

David has not been touched with tenderness for years, and it shows. He can run now, but he runs from those who love him and he hides in the toilet. He sits in the garden, ripping up the grass. Susan whispers to him, but he climbs a tree and sits there for three days, until she stops. The social worker talks about abuse and post traumatic shock and time. Matthew knows he is running out of time. He goes to his son and tells him how much he loves him and how much he missed him.

David laughs. 'You don't look like my father.'

Matthew knows what to do. He must make it like it was. He asks Leila to bake. Together they rebuild the house until its roof is marzipan, its windows are smoky with chocolate mist and its carpets are sticky toffee. Leila makes dumplings and her hands drip with syrup. Susan gives up after-school drama club and painting and says no to her first dates, for there's only time to eat. Matthew doesn't buy new clothes; he allows his belly to flop over tailored trousers so that David will see the memories that kept him alive. The family grow fat as moons and try to laugh like children.

Matthew watches David's face for happiness, for recognition. David is as round as the rest, but still his eyes are crumpled pieces of paper. He spends his days and most of his nights away from his family, and comes home with strange piles of money, no note smaller than twenty.

One day Matthew climbs into bed with David when he is asleep. He has a glass of warm milk in his hand. David is still dreaming, but he rolls on his tummy and presents his haunches, like a small dog waiting for mounting. Matthew vomits across Susan's books.

'I'm your father,' he says to David. 'I wouldn't touch you like that.'

David wakes up and laughs. 'Everyone has urges,' he says. 'I hear you at night with Mamma. I see the boys looking at Susan. Everybody touches me. Why not you?'

Matthew is his mother's little mud man. This is what she called him when he was very small, growing to be tall in the hills of Port Antonio in Jamaica.

Matthew goes for a walk by the river, and the fish cry. He watches the tourist men with the tourist women, slow-ripple waves filling his shallow eyes. He buys something in a shop and goes home to his family late at night. David is not there.

He wakes his wife softly and then lies on top of her, so that she cannot spark and burn him. The knife that he has bought is a sharp one and it slices through flesh easily. Matthew trims the hair between her legs first, and then cuts deeply and neatly, singing into Leila's cool ear. Matthew visits his daughter and does his work as fast as he can. He props Susan at the head of her bed and smiles at a job well done. He covers the bloody hole between her legs, and lays her down. She looks like she's dreaming.

Matthew slices onions and sweet peppers and seasons meat. He sets the table for one. He sits down and sharpens his knife. He can see his son in his mind, the men who touched him for so many years, and the men who still do. He tests the knife against his groin and readies himself for the pain. David can come home for dinner now. The home is pure. There will be nothing here to scare David, now. Nothing at all.

## AND YOU KNOW THIS

### *For Marjorie Ross*

Amber craned her neck, trying to see over the thick stream of passengers coming in at Terminal 3. There was still no sign of Birdie. She wondered if her friend was negotiating a hover frame after all. She was twenty minutes late, and who was late anymore?

When they'd spoken online two days ago, she'd found it difficult to conceal her shock at Birdie's tired eyes and thin face. Surely it wasn't that long since they'd connected, no more than a fortnight, both busy arranging things for the trip. But when she counted it was actually three weeks. Nearly four. Still, she hadn't expected Birdie to look so poorly. They'd both had their injections. Perhaps hers hadn't quite kicked in, yet.

'Is so me look bad?' Birdie had laughed at her expression.

'No, no, B,' Amber said, 'yuh look fine, girl.'

Birdie laughed again. 'After all these years yuh goin' start lie to me now?' Then she'd coughed for several minutes without pause, despite a glass of water, holding her chest and holding her side. That was when Amber had suggested the hover frame. After all, why did they pay their taxes if not for these little luxuries? All Birdie had to do was step out of the plane and be spirited to the airport lounge. A matter of seconds. But Birdie was as dismissive as she'd expected.

'Hover frame yuh rass! Is not *me* one ah mash up! After yuh have arthritis ah kill yuh off! Me can still dance yuh under the table – and yuh *know* this!'

Amber let herself laugh back. Whenever anyone spoke of Birdie they eventually winked and chorused: 'And yuh *know* this!' It was her stock phrase, stolen from some film in the 90s. Amber never could remember its name.

'Call for Sister Amber Bailey.' The cheery mechanical voice echoed through Arrivals. 'Sister Bailey, puh-leeze access Channel Number One Zero Three.'

She limped over to the Com Terminal. Birdie was right – she was a far cry from the dancer she had been. But just being out of a wheelchair was amazing. The lady who gave her the injection had embraced her when she took her first step. A kind woman, wearing eyeshadow far too blue for her complexion. The kind of young lady who threatened to ruin your coat collar with her concealer choices.

Amber flexed the fingers on her right hand – they still hurt like a macca bush, but she hoped that would pass soon – and slowly tapped in her code and gave her keyword to the operator. A recording reminded her that she was in Airport Jamaica 237 and wished her a spiritually productive day. On screen, silent waves stroked a peaceful shore. Amber rolled her eyes. They'd made it to 2070 and Com Terminal messages were still like those old telephone recordings: cheesy and insincere.

"Ey, gyal! Yuh deh-deh?' Birdie's face flickered on to the screen.

'Me here, man. Didn't I say I was coming?'

Birdie winked. 'Not like yuh have a choice!'

Amber kept the smile plastered to her face. 'So what taking so long? Man all over Jamaica waitin' for us!'

'Me comin', me comin'. Me jus' want to tell yuh de Medic goin' haffi give me another shot.'

That wasn't good.

'Two? Me barely did need di one. Yuh sure yuh don't need the hover frame?'

Birdie sucked her teeth. 'Me tell yuh a'ready – me come fi dance inna de sunshine. Jus' mek sure yuh have rum.'

The Com Terminal flickered into a peaceful blue. So much time and money had been wasted on the Big Blue Talks. Airport officials conferring with the wisest men and women in the world over their damn-fool Com Terminal screens. What low-octave frequency best to soothe tired travellers. And God, the months discussing the colour. Jamaicans were so damn high-chested. Still, in her day – she and Birdie's day she reminded herself – the government would have been too busy sending gunmen into local garrisons and thieving people money to spend time on the perfect shade of blue. Times had changed and she had to admit the screens did what they were supposed to do: she felt calmer, even after these few minutes, in front of one.

She walked back to Arrivals and smiled as a small, sprightly woman lowered her head respectfully, then jumped up to give her a seat.

'Peace be with yuh,' said the woman. She looked anxious.

'And also unto yuh,' Amber answered.

She watched the woman walk away, glancing backwards, like she, Amber, was a barking dog.

So. This was going to be how it felt.

''Ey gyal!'

Amber turned to see an open-armed Birdie coming towards her at a clip a fifty-year-old would admire. 'Yuh ready to mash down Jamaica?' People turned and stared. Same old Birdie. A bright purple, low-cut jumpsuit and orange stilettoes. She had tied yellow handkerchiefs all over her outfit – around her calves, dangling from her sleeves. The earrings were festive baskets of miniature fruit and her lipstick was uncompromisingly red against the ash of her face. Blue nails flashed on her hands. She'd always felt grey next to Birdie. She put a self-conscious hand up to her own tidy, braided hair, and then her friend was on her, hugging her.

She felt unexpected tears prick at her eyes.

'Lawd, girl, yuh look good, good, *good*!' Birdie patted her ass. 'Albert mussi cry *eye* water to see yuh out of that chair!'

'Some.' She didn't want to think about Albert right now; that was too hard. She wanted to smile as wide as she was smiling right now at Birdie. It had been too long.

Birdie read her mind. 'Ten years, eh? What a disgrace! Anyway, Miss Ting. We goin' mek up for it now! Where de car?'

One of the airport security guards showed them the way. She couldn't help wondering where he came from and how he was just a bit too damn smooth.

People passed them, whispering.

★

The convertible was sleek and mean, like a resting carnivore. They stood for a while, gazing at its green elegance, impressed. Birdie passed one long fingernail along its gleaming bonnet.

'Well, rass.'

Amber let out a breath. 'At least we got style.'

Birdie grunted. 'Yuh hands don' let yuh drive, right? So is me! Ah wonder how fast this t'ing can go?' She opened the door and climbed into the driver's seat, caressed the leather wheel, gazed at the dashboard. 'We can hit 500, chile! Zero to 500 in eight seconds!'

Amber carefully moved to the passenger side. The seat was soft and reassuring. 'Yuh know we not supposed to hit that speed until we reach,' she warned.

'That's no *fun*. Now. Tell me what's been goin' on with yuh.' Birdie hit a switch and watched delightedly as the top of the car slid away. She flung her arms open. 'Praise Jesus! Fresh Jamaican breeze!'

Amber opened her mouth to answer, but the sound of a child's voice interrupted her. A little girl on the pavement was tugging at her mother's hand, her high voice cutting through the air.

'Mamma, Mamma! Watch de Post Ladies! Post Ladies. Look Mamma! See dem deh!'

Her mother squirmed. 'Eleanor! Shut up yuh mout'!'

The child continued to stare at them, at the green car. 'But me never seen a Post Lady before. Me can talk to dem?'

Amber looked away. She had hoped to leave without this. It was too hard. She pressed her lips together.

The woman looked apologetic, gesticulated at her daughter. 'Me sorry. Peace be wid yuh –'

Birdie turned the key and the engine purred velvet. The way before them was clear and free. 'Lady! Tell yuh pickney –' she clicked to Start '– me not no *rass* Post Lady!' She put her foot down and threw her head back. The car leapt forward. 'Blooooddddd-claaaart!'

Despite herself, Amber began to laugh.

Their relic voices wound around each other, reminding them of their youth.

★

'Yuh want a draw?' Amber dangled the small packet at Birdie, watching her friend's long white hair stream back in the wind. Birdie had always been proud of her hair.

'What? Still a sinner!' Birdie chuckled. 'Tell me is double contraband!'

'Double double!'

They shrieked with laughter. Birdie closed the roof as Amber slipped a plastic case from her purse and began to roll the spliff on her knees.

'Damn expensive these days I hear…'

'Cheaper in the old days when it was illegal. Cho!' Amber tutted as the papers fell from her crumpled fingers. That injection was making her too optimistic.

'What?' Birdie was looking fine. There was a shine in her face.

'Nearly spill the damn weed all over the car.'

'Lord, hush, never mind!'

Amber turned her left hand over, blue lines in the back of it, lumpy thumb. Her hands were once quite beautiful. No-one said ugly, these days, but she thought it often.

'You save it?' said Birdie.

'Yes. Birdie?'

'What?'

She didn't want to be afraid. 'Yuh want to talk about it?'

'No.' There was a small silence. Birdie moved one hand from the steering wheel and patted Amber's cotton knee. 'Not yet, aright? Too soon.'

Amber bent forward and picked up the rolling paper. Pain flared on either side of her pelvis like two small probing knives. A small moan escaped from her lips.

Birdie glanced over, her face set. 'Yuh need to stretch, don't it?'

'Yeah.'

'We can take a first stop, soon.'

Amber realised that her blouse, so lovingly ironed by Albert that morning – Albert who still liked the old ways – was soaked with sweat. 'Me did tink the pain woulda done by now,' she said irritably.

'Too soon, baby.'

'Yuh think I shoulda tek a second injection?'

Birdie looked worried. 'One will do the job, them said.'

'Yeah, but yuh had two.'

'Keep pace with yuh.'

'Oh.' It hadn't occurred to her that co-ordination was necessary.

They were silent for a while. Birdie was something else – handling the green car like it was part of her body, scooping them through the Kingston traffic. Amber circled her wrists, stretched her crunchy elbows; stretched legs and circled ankles. The injection would probably improve things before the stretches did, but it helped to do something, however small. As she performed the exercises she thought about her daughter, Simone – her fit, efficient body. She and her husband always seemed to be bounding all over the place with their young children. Jogging, hiking, tennis, diving. That was good. She felt limited, a limiting grandparent. Worried she might frighten them with her chair, with her ugly.

Simone didn't approve. She'd come over from Quebec just before Amber left. Hardly spoke. Wouldn't stop stroking the curtains, palms wide and open. All over the house, stroking the heavy, burgundy curtains Amber had made when they first moved there, when Simone was a little girl. Her full mouth was set in a thin line when she left. She'd expected Simone to argue and fight. The silence was more disconcerting.

'Be positive,' said Birdie.

'What?'

'Yuh nuh hear the people-them say we must "remain positive"? Birdie sucked her teeth. 'Them did have one big-nostril man there, talking about how "mental attitude is key".'

Amber grinned. She set about rolling the spliff again. Sifting seeds, tiny bit of card; she could do it, now. 'What yuh *do* to him, Birdie?'

'Mi tell 'im the only thing that would really improve my mental attitude was a good backways-fuck.'

'What *happened*?'

'Well. Them fling me out of the group.'

'And then what?'

Birdie rolled her eyes. 'Then I charm my way back in, how yuh mean?'

When the weed was finally ready, the top went down again so they could swap it back and forth. Amber had brought a collection of their favourite oldies and Birdie insisted on turning the sound system to blaring decibels. Lionel Richie crooning. Prince promising them eroticity, Grandmaster Flash and the Furious Five. Amber surprised herself by remembering every lyric from 'The Message' and Birdie carolled out the chorus, her voice like steel inside cotton wool. They fought playfully over the rockers: who first, Chaka Demus & Pliers, or Shabba?

★

For lunch, they stopped at a bar at the side of the road. They had breached Kingston's outer limits and now thick trees caressed each other, breeding scarlet bougainvillea. Mosquitoes swam around Birdie's head as they exited the car.

'Boy. That weed gone straight to my head.' Birdie weaved slightly.

'Yuh could never hold a spliff.'

'Kiss me bumbo.' Determinedly, Birdie moved forward.

The bar was a modest affair, flanked by pink hibiscus bushes. Inside it was as cool as peppermint. Candy-striped chairs. No Vacupacked meals on the menu. REAL CURRY GOAT COOK LIKE YOUR MOTHER USED TO. The barman looked gloomy, but he brightened when he spotted the car.

'Peace be wid yuh.' It sounded strange in his mouth.

'That foolishness again?' Birdie rolled her eyes and parked herself on the stool in front of him. She wiggled her long fingers. 'Also unto yuh, an' gimme a rum an' coke. By de way, yuh have pan chicken?'

The barman shifted uncomfortably. Amber hid a smile. He was probably worrying about the bill. The government would award him several thousand points, of course. People were paid well to be good to Posts. Just that it would take at least six months to reach him. Blue screens hadn't solved bureaucracy.

He had the good grace to smile. 'Yes, ladies. We have chicken, curry goat –'

Birdie tossed that hair flirtatiously. So thick. 'What yuh want, Amber?'

Her stomach fluttered happily. '*Please* tell me yuh have a roti to put that goat into…'

His smile grew broader. 'You ladies know good food.'

Birdie arched her eyebrow. 'Well, look at how we old, man!' A tall frosted glass appeared before her. She took a long swig and shuddered. 'There is a God! Rass! Amber, park yuh pretty hide and put one of these down yuh neck! Mm, mm, *mmm*.'

Amber watched the man taking real onions from a container. He was no more than fifty. A spring chicken, and well preserved. Given his generation, he'd probably last until at least two hundred and fifty.

Birdie nudged her. 'Him sweet, eh?'

She shrugged. Thought of Albert. His voice, his polished shoes. His patient quiet.

Birdie raised her voice. 'Hey, Mr Bar Man! Me friend *like* yuh, yuh know!'

The man turned and grinned and then went back to chopping onions.

Amber writhed with embarrassment. 'Shut *up!*' she hissed.

Birdie would not be hushed. 'She want to know if yuh give a smooth ride, pretty man!'

'Sir, ignore me friend. De alcohol gone to her head.'

'Don' start me on the drink stories!' Birdie was in full swing. 'Me remember a *certain* somebody who get drunk di first time mi meet her and grab up two man one time! Don't look on dat innocent face and believe nutt'n, Mr Bar Man! No more than seventeen, a wine down wid two man! Slackness!'

Amber tried to put a hand up to Birdie's mouth, and they wrestled gently, playfully.

'Imagine…' Birdie was panting. 'Gyal, me seh, *let* me go! Imagine, Mr Bar Man, she married now, but me know seh Albert married her because the pu–'

'Birdie!'

'– me seh the *pum-pum* sweet him!'

Amber buried her head in her hands. She couldn't stop giggling. The bar-keep smiled at them. Together, they watched the laughter roll through the bright day and over the Blue Mountains.

★

'Birdie, which man yuh love the most in yuh life?' Forty minutes after they left the bar behind them, Amber had managed to lift her legs onto the dashboard and she left them there. It felt like victory. The car was going faster, and the wind splayed her plaits.

Birdie glanced at her. She had zipped her jumpsuit further down and her collar bones jutted into the wind. She downshifted to avoid a meandering chicken. 'Yuh can see seh we hittin' country. People out here still have dog and goat ah walk like people!' She yelled at the fleeing bird. 'Chicken! Yuh ever see a car in a hospital bed yet?'

Amber shook her head. 'Like yuh ever see a *chicken* inna hospital!'

'Wid de Animal Rights Bill in Atlanta yuh see dem all de time, me dear. Chicken wid bruk foot ah get aromatherapy; donkey dat forget how fe bray all ah get counsellin'–'

Amber burst into laughter. 'Birdie, how yuh so *lie*?'

'Yuh don' believe me? Me see fowl ah get rub down wid geranium oil!'

'Anyway, yuh changin' the subject.'

Birdie tossed her hair and sucked her teeth. 'Yuh know who.'

'Mickey?'

'Of course.'

Mickey. How could she forget? He was the only man who had ever made Birdie chase. They'd met in New York one long winter, the first time she and Birdie had lived in different cities. She in London, doing her nurse training, Birdie being Birdie, squired all over the US by a rich man thrice her age. In the days when Birdie's hair smelled so good you could get drunk on it. By the time she had scraped together the money to visit, Birdie had left the rich man and was drunk on Mickey. Mickey, who pulled out Birdie's hair in ten-strand handfuls, making her count. Mickey who brought Birdie a prostitute home for her twenty-first birthday. Insisted on watching. Sick Mickey, with toffee eyes. He'd lasted *too* long.

'But yuh lef' him... what? Seventy-eight, seventy-nine *years* ago...'

Birdie's laugh sounded younger than it had two days ago. 'Miss T'ing, ah don' really appreciate yuh remindin' me of me age!'

'Birdie...'

'A'right! Yes, me love him the most.' She flicked a fly off the steering wheel. The road had gone bumpy, rolling their breasts. 'The man had the sweetest lyrics me ever hear in me life. Would ah be wid him now? No rass way. Would ah tek him back fifty years ago? No. But sixty years ago, maybe. Maybe.'

'But why? He was an abusive *asshole*.'

'So yuh start swear now?' The car bumped. 'Somethin' just occur to me. Suppose dis car bruk down? What we do? Put it off?'

Amber moved uneasily. 'I guess we call dem an' dem send another one.'

They were silent once more, each lost in her own thoughts. Albert would be drinking a coffee substitute, hating it as he always did. It was still hard to be this age, with these memories, in these times. Remembering real coffee. He was only seventy-five. He could still have a life.

Love, even.

'Yuh know what?' Birdie's voice had moved down an octave.

'What?'

Birdie reached up. She did it so quickly that Amber had no time to register her intent. The hair, grey and black, sat in the purple lap. A wig. Amber stared. Birdie's naked skull was smooth and elegant. With all that hair in the way, she had never realised how graceful her friend's neck was. The sun spots didn't seem to matter.

'Oh my God! How long –'

'It start drop out fifteen years ago.' Birdie's voice was quiet. She coaxed the car up to 110. 'Is a'right. Old woman hair does drop out sometimes. But it mek mi t'ink ah Mickey. T'ink how him hurt me, an' how me woulda do anyt'ing for him dem time. So when it start drop out, mi shave it off.'

Amber touched the wig. It looked so real. It must have cost a thousand points. More. 'Birdie. Me don't know what fe tell yuh...' She wanted to cry.

'Fling it out for me, darlin'.'

'What?'

Birdie's jaw was set. 'Fling. Fling it out for me. Time for me to bloodclaaht realise seh me ah old woman!' Her voice rose. 'Yuh hear dat, Jamaica? Dis is a old woman, drivin' dis car! Too old fi fuckery!'

Amber could not remember a time when Birdie had looked so queer and so beautiful.

'Yuh sure?'

'Yes, girl. Fling it!'

Amber took a deep breath. Let the wig flow through her fingers into the tail wind.

★

The injection crept up on them, like the good weed had. She was sitting lotus-style, now. Hips free and smooth. They had told her to go slow, but if they hadn't been in this car she would have tried to dance. Like before she was a nurse. Drum. Pocomania. Wrap-head. *Grande jêté.* Rastafari *en pointe.* Now the hips were painless, she was suddenly aware of how many years she had been in pain. Curiously, she straightened her fingers. The ache was dying, creaked and subtle, an old rocking chair of sensation, clicking away from her.

'How yuh feel?' Amber asked.

'Wicked.' Birdie wriggled her slender hips in the seat. 'Me see seh yuh sittin' like one ah dem yoga man, like yuh bad.'

'It feel funny.'

'Dat's what dem seh would happen…'

'Yeah, but me forget what it feel like to not have to shift around de pain all the time, y'know? Yuh in pain a lot?'

Birdie tossed her head and then remembered she had no more hair to toss. 'Sometimes. Me nuh feel is cancer. Me t'ink some-body put a obeah spell on me.' She gripped the steering wheel. 'Yuh want to go faster?'

Amber was jolted out of her fascination with the fading discomfort.

'No. Not yet. How yuh in such a hurry?' She hated the sound of her voice. Squeaky and mean.

'Yuh 'fraid?'

'Well, is jus' like yuh can't wait to reach.'

Birdie squeezed her knee reassuringly. 'Me 'fraid too, girl. But what we goin' to do? Cyan' change it.'

★

Amber watched the deep green foliage whip past the edges of the car. They slipped across Flat Bridge and told each other the old stories of drownings, before they had made the bridge safe. Past Pum Rock, where matching sets of stone genitalia sat mysteri-ously in the rocks, one on each side of the river. They had proved them natural fifty years ago, after all the rumours that the indigenous Taino had created them. Amber giggled wildly. Pum Rock always pulled her funny bone.

It was she who had come back to Jamaica after her training. Birdie was the adventurous one, the one who had always wanted to see more, to get past what she saw as the parochial limitations of the island. Amber had missed everything about it in the four years she had been away. The dusty yellow butterflies that once a year took over Kingston, fluttering and dying on benches, in mid-air, on people's foreheads. The smell of anti-mosquito coils at night time as the heat dimmed and broke into soft orange-grey evening. The cut and thrust of Jamaican voices on the radio. Mango. Hairy mango and Number 7 mango. Bombay and Julie. Even as she watched things change, watched the whole world calm before her as people's spirits met and relinquished the old resentments, even as technology and spirituality had combined into a new order that she could not have predicted as a child, as shiny, efficient TransVacs replaced the clapped-out buses and the mad people disappeared from the streets, as Birdie wrote and then Skyped the news of her life, a life that had seemed inherently more exciting, with its stolen romantic hours. But she had not regretted staying in her country. The butterflies did not go away. Simone came back a few times a year with the family. She was proud of her daughter, a woman of her time, impatient but courteous in the face of her mother's archaic opinions. It was a good life with Albert's love and even his little miseries, even the arthritis and the heart condition they said they couldn't cure because she had old DNA. Her grandchildren would never have swollen joints or be unable to drive a car.

Amber felt warmth flow through her. It seemed to be concentrated in her legs. They said for each person it started in a different place. Started being Post. She unfolded a limb and gazed. The calf was strong, longer than she remembered.

Wondering, she reached out a hand, skin beaten brown and smooth. She hooked her skirt up to her thighs. For an odd moment she felt she was seeing her daughter's thighs from decades ago, but even as the thought occurred, she dismissed it. No. These were stronger. Dancer's thighs.

The warmth spread through and through.

'Amber...'

She looked across. Birdie's hair was growing back, like an animated black waterfall. It had started at her crown, wet sable. It was pouring its way down Birdie's back. But this was not the most astonishing thing. Birdie's face was changing. Fascinated, Amber watched the cheeks soften and fill, moulding around cheekbones that had become too sharp with alcohol and late nights and age. Birdie was shaking.

'It happenin', Amber? Ah can feel me face an' me body stretchin' –' Birdie took her eyes from the road and sucked her breath in sharply. Her voice was a whisper. 'Jesus Chris', girl! Yuh look like yuh twenty-one!'

Amber wrenched at the rear-view mirror on her side. The crow's feet were gone, spirited away like a dream. Unable to resist, she brought her hands down to the front of her blouse. Underneath the light material she could feel her heartbeat, hot beneath her skin.

'Oh my God, Amber – it really happen like dem seh, it really happen –'

Amber realised Birdie was near tears. The Emerald wavered dangerously on the slate road. So clean now, not like the rain-filled potholes of their childhood.

'Birdie, min' de car...' She felt as if she was speaking from a dream. They couldn't stop the car now. They had said they couldn't. She undid her blouse. Her breasts were heavy, like smooth sacks of wine. Somehow they had lifted themselves from their 101-year stoop and pressed back against her ribcage. She felt along the aureole, enjoying the wind on her naked flesh.

It was Birdie's tone that jerked her back into reality. She knew that sound. It was like when the headmistress had given them double detention and Birdie said she wasn't serving no detention; she had man waiting at the school gate. Her face had been set the same way: defiant and immortal.

She could feel the car slowing.

'Amber, ah stoppin' di car.'

A metallic voice emitted from the depths of the dashboard.

'Warning. Sister Bernadine Collins and Sister Amber Bailey. Warning. The Emerald T4 should not drop below two hundred miles per hour. You are not at the designated stage.'

Amber gripped her arm. 'Birdie, yuh cyan' stop! Remember? Birdie! Is soon time!'

Birdie shook her arm off. Her newly-young mouth was twisted. 'Ah goin' fin' somewhere to park. Who seh we cyan' jus' stop, eh? Who seh so? We could stop an' have it all over again. Dem couldn't find us!'

'Birdie, t'ink what yuh doin'! The car won't let yuh stop anyway! We would haffi jump!'

Birdie let go of the wheel. The green car exerted itself. The speedometer began to climb.

'Automatic drive now activated. You now have one hour to your final destination.' The mechanical voice was calm, but Birdie would not be soothed. All her hair was back, whipping richly against her face. Her eyes, Amber thought, were too bright. Birdie began to rise, one foot on the seat. She was trying to stand up.

Amber grabbed Birdie's leg, amazed at her own reflexes. She waited for a flash of pain. There was none. Only warmth. Birdie kicked awkwardly. She was yelling. The car was going faster.

'Nobody never try to get out! But *we* could! Look pon yuh! Look how yuh beautiful an' strong! Both ah we! Dem wouldn't fin' us! We could jus' disappear! Mek dem come find we inna bush!'

'No! No! Birdie! *Look* at me!'

Birdie struggled, trying to get away. 'Girl, if yuh don't want to jump, me goin' jump!' Amber held onto her with grim determination. Birdie felt like an electric eel. She had touched one at the beach when she was ten. It was a baby eel, crackling, but not enough to hurt. The wind whistled past her ears. The car was going faster.

'Birdie. *Listen to me*! If yuh jump out, yuh going to kill yuhself!' She had a handful of purple material. If she could just stop her from standing. She hooked her legs around the other woman's and tugged at the cloth with all her strength.

'*No –*'

'Birdie, ah beg yuh! Stay with me!' Amber yanked. Birdie, who had untangled a leg, crumpled. She half fell into Amber's lap, banging her hip on the gear shift. She began to cry. Amber stroked her hair. It was soft. Softer than any expensive wig. Birdie's mascara was running. She still used mascara. Old time ways. She raised her face. Amber marvelled at the symmetry. She had old photographs of them together that Simone laughed at. She had thought they captured Birdie's face. None did.

'We only have one hour, Birdie.' She didn't know what to say.

'Yuh remember de butterflies in de school yard?'

'*No.*'

'Yeah, man. Yuh remember. Yellow butterflies. Like clouds. A whole heap ah dem. Dem used to fall on yuh face an' dead. An' yuh would get vex.'

She smiled as Birdie chuckled into her shoulder.

'Yes. An' yuh would look like yuh goin' to bawl, cause yuh know dem was goin' to dead.'

'Yes.' They rocked together for a little while. The Emerald purred on.

Birdie touched her own face. 'Is only dat me get excited, y'know.'

'Ah know.'

'Yuh know me did always like me looks. Me admit it, me kinda vain. An' de idea dat me coulda have it all again. Y'know. Walk down street wid dis body, mek de man dem call out…'

'Dem nuh even whistle dese days, Birdie. Dat is old time behaviour.'

'Me know, me know. Just dat ah miss bein' beautiful. Ah miss man cryin' at me foot bottom. Yuh have a husband. Him 'memba how yuh used to look. Me nuh have nobody. Jus' de woman dem inna me building, an' dem all t'ink me mad…'

Amber looked at her. 'But dem not wrong.'

They laughed.

'But yuh undastan', right?' Birdie said.

'Of course,' said Amber.

The metallic voice interrupted them. 'Sister Bailey and Sister Collins. You have fifty minutes to final destination. Countdown will begin one minute before arrival. Peace be unto you.'

Birdie pulled herself upright. She put her head on one side and reached across to hold Amber's hand. They chorused together.

'*And we know this!*'

★

They watched the clock, listening to the sound of their own breathing. Amber thought that she had never really heard her own breath before. Even when meditation and breathing exercises had become compulsory at school, and she'd had to do catch-up lessons with Simone. Albert would pinch her and tell her she didn't have a damn thing to catch up on – new-fangled indulgences.

When she walked out of the house this morning she had not looked back at his tears.

'Well.' Birdie shook herself. 'Since me get back me hair an' de car doin' it own bloodclaaht t'ing, ah goin' step inna de back seat an' blow inna de breeze.'

'Do *not* jump,' Amber said.

'Me learn me lesson.' Birdie's voice was contrite.

It was wondrous to see her clamber skilfully across the seats, like she was sixteen again. Amber leaned against the back of the car seat and gazed at her. The purple jumpsuit bagged at the waist and hugged too closely at the hips. It was three inches too short. Birdie had shrunk with age. Amber looked at herself in the mirror again. They had warned her that it could be confusing, disorientating, but she felt quite calm. She had never been too fond of her face anyway, supposed that it had served her, but that was all.

The car continued to purr around sharp lanes. It was getting faster. She took a deep breath and followed Birdie into the back.

Birdie tried to smile at her, her ribcage rising and falling. She was trying not to hyperventilate, trying to talk.

'Who yuh – who yuh –'

Amber took Birdie's hands in her own. Part of her felt serene, as if none of it was happening.

'Calm down, sweetie. What yuh want to seh?'

Birdie gulped and her breathing steadied. 'Who yuh love the most in your life?' she said. The Emerald whizzed along the road. The engine sounded as if it was speaking to them.

*Nearly there nearly there nearly there nearly there.*

Amber smiled. 'Albert, of course. And Simone.' She looked away. She had hoped there would be no questions for her. It was one of the reasons she had chosen Birdie. A ride full of her oldest friend's confessions, regrets, denouement. Then she could hide her own thoughts.

'Me nuh believe yuh.' Birdie struggled to sit up. Even her voice had changed. Back to the sweet tones of their high school choir.

Amber looked at the clock. Twenty minutes. And counting. She could see the sparkle of the water by the road. They were by the sea and it wouldn't be long.

'Sing fo' me, Birdie,' she said.

'I will. Just tell me. Tell me who yuh love the most. Me know is not Albert. Every woman have a firelight in her eye fe the man who sweet her, lif' her up. An' yes, me know seh yuh love Albert. An' me know yuh choose me because me woulda talk de head off a donkey. But is your time too, Amber. An' me fling-weh my hair a'ready.'

Amber shook her head. All the nights of regrets, sleepless, longing. She had pretended for years.

'Tell me which man yuh love the most.'

Amber laughed. It was a silver sound, lost in the wind and the unending mutter of the engine. She listened to the warmth running through her. One plait looped over her shoulder. No grey. Perhaps it was time to tell. They'd said she should not reach her destination bound by silence. She turned to look at Birdie with her soft throat and her kiss-me-yuh-fool lips and her dark, wise skin, almost purple, like the tree bark around her mother's house.

'Is yuh.' The words sat between them. She felt as if something had broken inside her newly sixteen-year-old self. 'Me love yuh since me meet yuh.'

Birdie's face was a mixture of horror and incredulity.

'Me love yuh since me see yuh ah cuss wid teacher in de school yard. Love yuh all de time, Birdie. Sleep over wid yuh ah night time, ah giggle 'bout man, tell yuh how fe kiss dem.' She closed her eyes as the warmth plunged and rose in her. 'Remember how me tell yuh how fe kiss?'

'Put yuh mout' on him mout', soft up yuh lip an' memba fe breathe.' Birdie sounded as if she was reciting.

The clock blinked at them.

'Me never want to tell yuh now. Me never want it to be de las' t'ing yuh memba 'bout me. Mek yuh t'ink seh me ah watch yuh an' t'ink bad t'ings… but de injection – it makin' me warm.' She giggled. It was like being happily drunk. 'What a rass injection!'

Birdie put her hands up to her eyes. 'But why yuh married? Why yuh lie? Why yuh never talk, baby? Dis is de time fe people recognise dem t'ings. Dem wouldn't judge yuh. Not like when we was pickney.'

Amber laughed again. 'Cause is only yuh, Birdie. An' me did know seh yuh wouldn't love me back.'

The Emerald smoothed its body around the corner. The sea flirted with them from a distance. Soon they would be on the sand. They could feel its urgency. The speedometer began to rise.

Birdie was crying.

'Yuh 'fraid, Birdie?' She reached out for her hand. 'Yuh 'fraid?'

Blue nails dug into her fingers.

'No. Is not 'fraid. Is yuh, girl. Me cyaan stan' it. Jesus Chris'! So yuh regret everyt'ing, yuh waste everyt'ing!'

Amber shook her head. She must make her understand. She had to yell over the wind. Streams of sand whirled around them, golden clouds.

'All me did want to do was tell yuh. Dat's all. Me live me life. Nuh regret nuttin'.' She searched Birdie's wet eyes. 'Tell me yuh know what me mean. Me a'right. Me did jus' wah tell yuh.'

'Me nevah *know*! Me never *give* yuh anyt'ing!'

Amber reached out and it felt as if Birdie floated into her arms. Belly to belly. 'Yuh was me friend, B. Dat's all. Dat's good.' The car roared and she felt her heart beating. Like a yellow butterfly.

'Sing for me, Birdie,' she said.

Birdie raised up her voice. It was strong and long and real. An old hymn. From hot days in Sunday school.

'You are the rose, the rose of Sharon to my heart…'

The sand obliterated the car. It was as if they were lost in a quiet storm.

'You gave me water that refreshes me in every part… you are so beautiful…'

The sand changed around them. Kaleidoscope colours, bright as a bird's wing filling their eyes. They held tight. And Birdie sang.

'And I love you more than words can say…'

Amber's final moment of consciousness was filled with the sound of Birdie's voice, filling her eardrums as the Emerald thundered towards the Light.

'You are my beloved and my happiness in every way…'

★

The little girl smiled hesitantly at her mother as they sat cross-legged on warm mats in the bedroom. The last of the illuminations were fading into the distance. It was the third time they had seen them in as many weeks.

'Mamma, yuh think those lights were for the Post Ladies we saw today?'

'Probably.' Her mother reached out to touch her face. 'It mek yuh sad, Ellie?'

'No. Dem look old an' happy.'

'Ah t'ink dem was well happy.' Her mother helped her into bed.

The child listened to her mother's footsteps on the stairs. She smiled at the window as the purple lights flittered into night and a final golden bubble sank beyond the window into the sea.

## MASKI-MON-GWE-ZO-OS
## [THE TOAD WOMAN]

Maski-mon-gwe-zo-os sells the fatty, yellow lotion she harvests from her back and arms. She's bald. Her legs are long, her lips pendulous. She wraps fragrant cedar belts around her distended belly and stores the lotion inside those terrific lips – beside tracts on divorce, contraceptives, homeopathic painkillers, abortifacients and tiny knives, such as a woman might slip up her sleeve on the night-bus.

'Look at her leaping,' they say. Soaring over men's heads, knickerless, her breasts buoyant sacks in the breeze. She's never killed a man, despite the warrant out for her arrest. When brave children ask what the warrant is for, Maski-mon laughs.

'They don't like the sound of my voice,' she says. 'But come, let us sing, anyway.'

## ACKNOWLEDGEMENTS

*The Woman Who Lived In A Restaurant* as a limited edition chapbook, ed. Nicholas Royle (Nightjar Press, Oct 2015) and in *Best British Stories 2016*, ed. Nicholas Royle (Salt, Autumn 2016)

'The Mullerian Eminence' in *Closure*, ed. Jacob Ross (Inscribe/Peepal Tree Press, UK: London, Autumn 2015)

'Fix' in *The World To Come*, ed. Om Dwivali (Australia: Melbourne, Spineless Wonders, July 2014)

'Smile' in *Minuteman*, 1st edition, ed. 12 (Awe & The Abyss, April 2013)

'Roll It' in *Kingston Noir*, ed. Colin Channer (Akashic Books: USA, May 2012)

'Love Silk Food' in *The Best British Short Stories 2011*, ed. Nicholas Royle (UK: Salt Publishing, October 2011) and in *Wasafiri* magazine, eds. Bernardine Evaristo and Karen McCarthy (USA, September 2010)

'The Heart Has No Bones' in *Incommunicado*, eds. Romy Ashe and Tom Doig (Australia: Express Media, May 2006)

'Breakfast Time' in *Tell Tales, The Anthology of Short Stories*, Vol. 2, eds. Rajeev Balasuramanyam and Courttia Newland (London: Flipped Eye Publishing Ltd., June 2005)

'Breathing' in *Spoonface: A Collection of Short Fiction*, ed. Clem Cairns (Ireland: Fish Publishing, 2004)

'President Daisy' in *The Writer Fellow: An Anthology,* Oscar Wilde Centre at Trinity College Dublin, Ireland 2004)

'Art, for Fuck's Sake' in *Brown Sugar 2*, ed. Carol Taylor (USA: Simon & Schuster, December 2002)

'Covenant' in *Whispers in the Walls: Black and Asian Voices*, eds. Leone Ross & Yvonne Brissett (UK: Tindal Street, 2001) and in *Obsidian III: Literature in the African Diaspora*, ed. Kwame Dawes (USA: North Carolina State University Press, 2001)

'Drag' in *Brown Sugar: A Collection of Erotic Black Fiction*, ed. Carol Taylor (USA: Dutton Plume, January 2001)

'Mudman' in *Time Out London Short Stories, Vol. II*, ed. Nicholas Royle (USA & UK: Penguin, 2000)

'Phone Call to a Rape Crisis Centre' in *Burning Words, Flaming Images*, ed. Kadija Sesay (UK: SAKS Media, 1996)

## ABOUT THE AUTHOR

Leone Ross is a critically-acclaimed Jamaican/British writer. Her short stories have been anthologised in the UK, USA, Australia, Canada and Slovakia. Her story "Love Silk Food" was placed second in the 2009 V.S Pritchett Award and a smaller version of this collection, *Lipstick Lighters, Pens & Porn* was shortlisted for Scott Prize (Salt) in 2011. Her novels are *All The Blood Is Red* (ARP, 1996) and *Orange Laughter* (Anchor, 2000). In 2010, *Wasafiri* magazine named *Orange Laughter* one of the most influential novels in the last 25 years. Ross' upcoming third novel is called *This One Sky Day*. She is a Senior Lecturer in the Department of English and Creative Writing at Roehampton University, London.